# TALES FROM THE REALM

## VOLUME ONE

Aphotic Realm

Owners | Editors: Dustin Schyler Yoak & A.A. Medina

Associate Editor: Chris Martin

Art Director: Gunnar Larsen

**Tales from the Realm, Volume One**

Edited by: Dustin Schyler Yoak

Cover Art: "Tales From The Realm: Part One" | Original Artwork by Gunnar Larsen



www.AphoticRealm.com



ISBN: 1717398170
ISBN-13: 978-1717398178

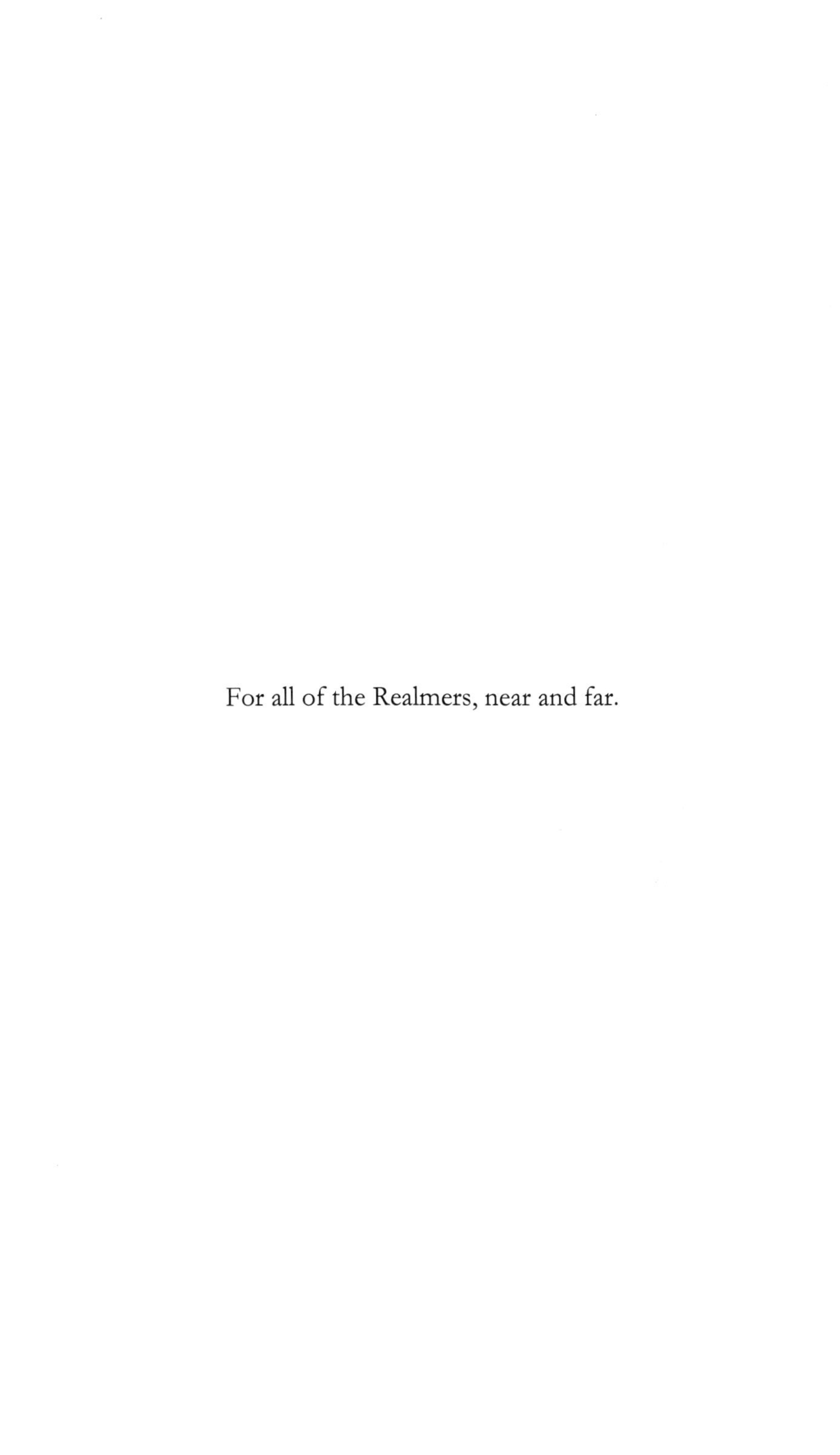

For all of the Realmers, near and far.

# CONTENTS

Thank you to all the authors for believing in what we are doing and supporting our publication by continuing to submit fantastic stories.

# FOREWORD

Somewhere far beyond your reality, is a plane of darkness, home to strange and sinister beings with twisted imaginations and senses of humor. That is where you find yourself today. Welcome to the Aphotic Realm.

Before A. A. Medina and I even created and named this refuge for like-minded beings such as you and I, we knew we wanted to do a "Best of Collection" and gather stories by year. As 2017 wound down, we only encountered one problem with that desire, how do we select the "best of" something when every story is fantastic and every author the very definition of exceptional?

The answer, we decided, is that you really don't. I decided that the only way to proceed was to have each member of our team list out some of their favorites. From there, I collected the Tales before you now. I selected as wide a sampling as possible: we've got monsters, murderers, fairies, tortured souls, and more. I also made sure to get a sampling of as many of the genres/sub genres of which we've received submissions.

I hope you enjoy this collection, as it represents some of the best stories Aphotic Realm had to offer in 2017. Stay strange and stay sinister, Realmer!

Thank you,
Dustin

A. A. Medina, Dustin Schyler Yoak, Chris Martin and Gunnar Larsen - Your Aphotic Realm Team

# SILENCING THE BELL

GARY BULLER

Harry Stubaker's ritual had become an addiction, like the booze, but somewhere inside he knew this would be the final time. He reached for his glasses on the bedside table, ran a clammy palm down his chin and pulled the duvet away. Fully clothed, he wore blue jeans and a Gingham shirt. He rose from the mattress and looked out of the window. It was mid-December and snow had blanketed the entire estate overnight, glistening atop the bird table on his back lawn.

*Brrrring, Brrrrring.*

His eyes found a structure in the darkest corner of the garden, close to the brick facade of the house. Had the sun been shining, he would have seen a windowless shed. Ageing and weather-bleached, rusting nails and screws barely held it together. The wood was untreated and had begun to peel and warp in places. He sighed and descended the stairs, where a kitchenette led to the back door.

He brewed a cup of coffee, the stale granules tasting like dishwater and stared absently at a family photograph, a spider-web of cracks in the glass. The papers awarding custody of their son to Shirley lay on the kitchen table. Harry looked at his grazed knuckles, knowing he was delaying the inevitable. The terrible shrine called to him.

Sandra was right. He was worthless.

*Brrring, Brrring.* The bell rang again. Impatient. Anticipating.

Hot coffee spilt onto Harry's wrist and he cursed under his breath. Slipping into a pair of Wellingtons, cold against the holes in his socks, he opened the door to the freezing night. His foot sank through the top layer of frozen flakes with a crunch. It was twelve inches thick, and he guessed by the weighty clouds above, more was on its way.

*Brring. Brrring, brrring.*

Much louder now, though the snow had a strange muffling effect, wrapping the sound in cotton wool. Even the nearby motorway was oddly muted. He thought about the cherry-red car residing on his driveway, as it had for the past twelve months. How Sandra's eyes narrowed when he told her the engine was knackered. He imagined she smelled the lies on him, as she smelled beer on his breath.

A flake of snow, no bigger than a fingernail kissed the round of his cheek and rolled downwards like a tear. It was the first of many as the sky came alive. The houses and trees around him gradually faded behind a white veil.

Pausing at the shed door, he hesitated. In his periphery, beyond the garden gate, the unlit headlights of his car stared judgmentally beneath drooping lids of snow. A dog barked twice and then fell silent. He unlocked the rickety door and tugged it open against a drift of snow. The interior was black and frigid. Plumes of moist air floated from Harry's mouth in rhythm with the throbbing in his temples. His shoulders slumped under a great weight.

*Brrring.*

A breath froze in his throat and he stood, statuesque. He squinted into the murk, praying he wouldn't see the face from his nightmares. There was a strange electricity in the air, like he wasn't alone and he convinced himself the shuffling and scraping was just the wind blowing in the eaves. Shaking, his fingers reached for the toggle by the door, finding air once, twice before finally grasping the cord. The bulb blinked into existence, emitting a thin light.

Shadows chased into nooks and recesses, but the strange electricity stayed.

Harry inhaled deeply.

There it was.

A spindly frame reclined in the furthest corner. The front tyre was flaccid and misshapen. Spokes jutted outwards like a fistful of knitting needles. Harry sipped on his coffee, regretting it wasn't something stronger. Remembering. The past replayed on loop, like an upended, spinning tyre. Each time, he tried to change what he'd done and each time he failed.

***

A man bent over a glassy pathway, pouring salt from a sack. Next to him, a woman in a thick coat raised a hand to protect her eyes from the low, winter sunshine. The temperature was sub-zero, but Harry's nose and ears were warm. He studied the couple as he drove by, his eyes sluggish in his mildly inebriated state.

Later, he used an abrasive sponge to scrub the frame, convinced he saw blood until he realised it was flecks of paint from his Ford. In many ways, he thought this was much worse.

***

Chunks of foam protruded from the torn seat and the handlebar resembled the limbs of an ancient tree, twisted and scuffed. Only the bell, clasped to one handle, was unaffected by his actions. It rang just before impact and had not stopped ringing since.

"What do you want from me?" he asked, eyes stinging.

"*What do you want?*"

***

Powerless to stop the nightmare unfolding, the couple froze. The bag of salt hit the pavement and they both sprinted toward the gutter. Here, a small, mannequin-like figure lay still. They screamed her name again and again, like they were losing their minds.

The rear wheel, spinning in the air with a clickety-clack of spokes, was his tenuous anchor to reality. As the gravity of the situation sunk in, he understood the bicycle was also evidence. Harry wasn't proud of what happened next. It was a shameful thing to do.

"I have too much to lose..."

Before he realised what he was doing, the bike was on

his back seat and he'd slipped the car into first gear.

The father spoke into his mobile phone with short, breathless snatches.

"Yes... ambulance please... hurry... please hurry... not breathing..."

His wife knelt in the snow, cradling a pale face that stared blankly at the sky. Neither of them had processed the idea someone else was involved, yet. Bile lurched up Harry's throat. He had to get out of there. The car sped off, clipping one pavement side-on, as he momentarily lost control on a patch of ice.

In Harry's rear view mirror, the father waved urgently in his direction. He made a few faltering steps towards the rapidly departing car, then glanced back and stopped.

"*Shitshitshitshit,*" Harry hissed. The heat rose in his face, but he had never felt as sober in his life. He turned right onto the slip road and pressed hard on the accelerator, joining the other motorway traffic. Somewhere in the brisk winter air, he thought he heard the wail of sirens. Taking the first exit, the Ford Escort pulled into a disused multi-storey car park. He sat while the engine idled, wondering what he was going to do next.

***

Their marriage wasn't quite on the rocks but had been dangling over the precipice for some time. Harry often brought his frustrations home from work, where he produced filter tips for cigarettes. Evening meals became fractious and awkward, especially when he brought a four-pack to the dinner table. Then he stopped coming home and went to the Red Lion instead.

"You're never here anymore, physically, or up there." His wife said, finger pointed to her temple. How could he argue with that? It was the beginning of the end.

The bicycle, or his feverish concealment of it, was a rotten seed taking root in his home, destroying everything from the ground up. He thought about dumping it at the tip, under cover of darkness, but what if someone found it? Destruction of the bicycle didn't seem right. Especially when news reports told him the child had died. Instead, Harry concealed the bicycle under a ground sheet at the back of the shed. His wife wouldn't find it because she didn't have a key.

Harry would have said the ringing started on the day his wife left him, except this wasn't entirely true. He thought he heard a bell pealing in his nightmares, and then later, as he lay awake in bed. Initially, he blamed the alcohol, but quickly came to realise it was the ghost of his past calling out to him. When his wife and son left, taking with them their belongings, he didn't bother to cover the bicycle anymore.

***

Harry stood on a three-legged stool and retrieved a white bottle from a shelf. It had the black silhouette of a rodent on the label.

*Brrring, Brrring.*

He stepped down, turning to the twisted metal frame.

"I know, I'm so sorry. I shouldn't have been driving. I should have handed myself in. I'm so tired, so bloody tired."

Taking a deep breath, he placed a palm on the handlebars. They were cold enough to burn. He imagined that deep underground, at Smithill Cemetery, it was very cold too. "I'll do right by us," he said, casting his eyes to the floor. He moved to the doorway, and with a final look back, pulled the toggle.

Outside, the snow fell slowly, obliterating his footsteps. Goose-feather flakes drifted all around, settling on his shirt, arms and head. He barely noticed.

Snow collapsed from his car bonnet with a wet *schlup*, exposing the damaged front bumper, and scarred paintwork. To Harry, the grooves were as deep and dangerous as a yawning chasm.

***

The Ford Escort was one of the reasons he eventually lost his job, at least that's what he told himself. He dared not drive the car at risk of someone noticing the damage, he wouldn't visit a mechanic for the same reason. It stayed on the driveway at the side of his house, only visible from the rear gate. He caught the bus to work, but not long after Shirley left, he would disembark outside the Red Lion.

"You're a no-good drunk; you know that Stubaker?" his supervisor once said.

He supposed his supervisor was right.

Harry re-entered the kitchenette, remembered that he hadn't brought his mug and shrugged. Taking a fresh one, he boiled the kettle for a second time and tipped a generous helping of pellets from the white bottle. He thought for a moment and then added some more. A green sludge foamed as he poured in the hot water.

The vapours drifting from the dissolved pellets smelled chemical. They made his eyes stream, but Harry knew what he had to do. The television appeals said the hit and run killer had yet to be found, and called for the culprit to hand himself in. The child's parents couldn't remember the make or model of the car involved, but they both agreed it was cherry red.

Harry Stubaker lifted the cup to his lips.

*Tap, tap, tap, tap, tap.*

Floorboards above creaked as small steps made cautious progress.

His eyes traced the ceiling; a pause here, the groan of wood there, like it was searching. Gooseflesh blossomed across Harry's shoulders and down his arms.

He should be alone, but he wasn't.

"Hello?"

Silence descended.

Harry held his breath, sure someone upstairs was listening. Even the slightest sound would be heard, and that was bad. Time passed in the darkness. His eyes bulged, and lungs burned-screaming to exhale.

He just had to.

Harry let out a slow, faltering breath.

The steps resumed, quicker now. Eagerly, they crossed the threshold of the room above and out onto the landing. They *bump, bump, bumped* down the stairs, towards him, gathering pace. He sidestepped, looking out into the hallway where the bottom step was visible- but saw nothing. They continued, the sound of small shoes crossing the black and white tiles, increasing in volume and intent.

He wasn't quite sure what happened next.

The bulb above flickered and then died, plunging him into a milky blue darkness.

"Hello?" he asked, praying no reply came.

The mug yanked forcefully from his fingers and smashed against the far wall. Green slime spilled down the tiles. Stunned, he looked this way and that but saw no-one.

*Ring-ring, Ring-ring.*

On the verge of panic, it took a moment to register it was the hallway telephone. Harry weaved around pieces of broken porcelain and raised the handset. For a moment, he could hear nothing but the thump of his heart.

"Hello?"

The line clicked a *tap, tap, tap* as if the connection was fragile.

"Hello, this is Harry Stubaker, can I help you?"

A stilted inhalation- as if the person whom he was speaking to had been crying, and was struggling to catch their breath. Harry's heart stopped in his chest.

"H-Hello?"

"Mr Stubaker?"

A small voice emerged from behind the curtain of

static and then withdrew. Harry didn't know if it was male or female, but it was certainly a child.

*The* child. Colour drained from his winter-worn cheeks.

"Hope?"

He knew the name well, from television news reports and the front page of newspapers. Suddenly the faltering, searching sounds upstairs made sense. He kept neatly clipped articles about the accident in a shoe box under his bed, and it was looking for them.

“Hope, I’m so sorry.”

The line died, and a strange, suffocating atmosphere settled around him. He missed the cradle of the receiver twice, before dropping the handset to the floor. Diminutive footsteps rounded the corner from the kitchenette.

A semi-transparent figure emerged, distorting the lines of the door frame, and stalked towards Harry. Two arms reached out to him, her mouth open in a silent scream. Harry's eyes widened, and his blood turned to ice. It was her.

He turned and ran, grabbing the handle of the front door and out onto the pathway. The shape pursued him into the emerging dawn. Harry's boots slipped on a patch of ice hidden under the powdery snow. He almost fell, but regained balance and continued onto the street. Insanely, the bell pealed again and again, though from this distance it should have been impossible to hear.

The figure was upon him, Harry could feel it like an icy draft at his back.

Then the truck hit him.

***

George Bradley had worked at the furniture delivery company for only three days when the accident happened. The sat-nav had been unreliable from day one, sending him on convoluted routes through small towns and down one-way streets. A simple motorway trip would have done a more efficient job. That morning, it was taking the biscuit. George was sure he was heading in the wrong direction, through this random housing estate- it transpired he was correct.

He tapped the touch screen, squinting at the tiny icons.

The lorry collided with the man, throwing him into the air like a rag doll.

George slammed on the air-breaks with a hiss, his mind a jumble of panic and confusion and climbed down from the cabin. The snow was thick, and he trudged through the drifts to the unmoving body. He could have sworn the man had been looking over his shoulder when the impact occurred.

An open door led into a scruffy looking dwelling. George saw one set of footsteps in the snow, but shuddered. It looked like the man was being chased. He rang emergency services. As he spoke to the dispatcher, he thought he heard something, and looked to the house again. He frowned and shook his head. *No, it doesn't make sense.*

"Are you still on the line, Mr. Bradley?" the dispatcher asked.

"Yes, I'm here," he replied. "The house seems to be empty, but I thought I heard a bell."

## About the Author

Gary Buller is an author from Manchester England where he lives with his partner Lisa, daughters Holly & Evie and dog Chico. He grew up in the Peak District where the hauntingly beautiful landscapes inspired him to write. He is a huge fan of all things macabre, and loves a tale with a twist. He is a member of the Horror Writers Association.

Twitter @garybuller
Website: www.garybuller.com

# OTHER MOTHER

SKYE MAKARIS

The king's cock was small. Much too human. Small and cold and hard, a swede of ice lashed to his hips. He grunted and squirmed: just like that, his part was finished. He nodded me away, and I retired to my moors to begin the creating.

He wasn't the first king I served. His great-great-grandsire had shared my bed, a hundred years ago and change, but this was different. This was duty.

The queen's insides were lumpen, she told me, in a whisper laced with a sob. She had tried for years already, and couldn't I see how her hair was growing grey? How her brow creased where once gaiety had dwelt?

"I need an ersatz womb," she whispered. She worried her hands in shame.

I reached forward to clasp her trembling palms. "What's mine is yours," I said, and kissed her cheek.

***

*What's yours is mine*, I thought when the king presented his cock. He wasn't an ugly man, but he wasn't his grandfather. Great-grandfather? How long had it been? A human lifespan and then some, cold and puckered with loss, since I'd had him. Mothers on mothers on mothers of mine had kept his line's counsel. Lent our ears and our arms and our keenness for strategy to a family near as ancient as ours. It was the way of kings back then: keep the fair folk close to your breast, and we'll proffer loyalty no human can summon. That was then.

***

When he first unlaced my stays, that man of mine, my mother rang harshly in my mind. Keep that man out of your bed, idiot child. Keep humans out of your heart. They are beautiful, cursory, all too slight, and one day they will die and you will be tempted to follow.

She was right. He shriveled, while I continued to bloom. His faculties shrank while mine grew shrewder. He died, and I keened sharply. And then I peeled myself from his graveside and went to attend his son. That was then.

Now son of son (of son?) lay beside me, giddy with my gift to him. What's yours is mine--indeed.

***

Soon I summoned them to feel the quickening. My belly was bright and bold: the seed inside was knitting, and briskly at that. When the queen laid her hand against it, my dear friend gasped and sang.

"He will be strong," I promised. "You won't find a better stopgap womb anywhere. His blood will be rich and sweet. His bones will be sturdy. His hair will be spider silk; his eyes, sea. A faery's body is the best first home a child could want. You have chosen well."

My queen's eyes were shining. She took my hands in hers. Her husband gripped my shoulder.

"But he *will*, of course, be a he?"

***

She was not a he.

I hit my throes early. The babe still had another month to go. When I felt the sluices open, I was delighted. I had spent eight months succoring the child, making him strong and fair, a man with roots in each world. A man with the salt of his father's people and the glamour of mine. It was only fitting he should arrive a month too soon. He would be his own man from the very first breath.

For an hour and a day I labored, but the bearing was easy: we are our own race, informed by our own gods, our own bloodlines our own flesh our own memory, and we do not share Eve's curse. My dear friend the queen was there to knead my back and kiss my forehead.

"What's mine is yours," she whispered as my belly rippled. "We will never forget what you have done for us—for our kingdom, for *me*. I promise he will know us both, you as well as I. He will always love his faery godmother, who gave her body to the service of our bloodline."

With a final howl, the babe unleashed himself. The queen sobbed with glee while the nurses toweled off the squirmling. And then I watched my dear friend's joy sour, her color sink to grief, for the squalling heir was soft and pink and all too feminine.

The room grew cold as the nurses prodded her. The queen was silent. Her chin was harsh, her eyes dark and sour. I petted my goddaughter's head. Her lips cooed back at me, demanding love. A princess in perfect miniature. Begging, hoping, I offered her to the woman who had promised to be her mother. And my dear friend turned her head away.

"You *promised*," she said, when she could speak. "A son spun of spider silk and sea. A boy in his father's image. Instead you bear us...this. A half-breed daughter who will never rule, never own, never wear the crown her blood deserves. You might as well drown her yourself, for all the good she'll do us."

She straightened, but her back was still sloped with grief. I couldn't speak. My legs were still spread, my brow striped with sweat, and the girl in my arms was beginning to writhe. I could feel my blood stirring in her barely-body, and I understood all at once.

The queen, that dear petty striving conniving woman, would not be outshone. A faery son would be joy itself, pride in a glowing skin, but a faery daughter would always dull her mother. Just the wrong side of mortal brilliance. She would be, forever, a brighter coin. In the presence of her birth, my dear friend had already begun to crumble.

I observed her, but I could not act. I was still lashed to

my childbed, witted but weak. I let her scoop up the child she could not love.

"She will be ours," said the queen. "She was never yours, and your word will be sullied should you ever speak else. She will never be fae. Never more than her human flesh implies. When the time comes, she will marry the man we choose and forget she ever bore another name. Good riddance to half-breed rubbish."

***

They called her Aurora, I heard. A tribute to the morning sun. I laughed when I heard, the better to keep from crying. This from a mother who could not abide her daughter's shine. I was not invited to the christening. I tossed and turned that night: that was *my* flesh asleep in the cradle, *my* blood bubbling behind those pretty eyes.

Did she know who her grandsires were? Did she know she'd been born too late? *If your father had been him, my love instead of my duty*, I sang one night, hoping she could hear, hoping our blood might carry bits of magic to her bones and guts and brain, *you would know what you are.*

I grieved her faithfully. I grieved the loss of my queen's dear friendship, and I grieved my dismissal from the king's counsel. Mothers on mothers on mothers untold had advised the royal line. I had shamed us all. I had lost a history and a daughter in one. I had lost.

***

I went back to my moors. My people asked no questions. I took a lover among my own stock. Waking up beside him was almost good enough. He didn't ask me questions. He was warm and measured, tender when he needed to be. We lived in my mothers' mothers' moorland home. Hunted for our food, studied for our craft, built something that looked like a life.

Sometimes when the moon was jaunty, leering a little too close to the night of my princess's birth, I stormed. My home was haunted, they started to say. I heard whispers of spirits and spooks, of ghouls and ancestral wails: no, just me. Me and the sprinklings of magic I sloughed off when it all grew too much, a private palaver between my grief and me. Braids of lightning attended my walls. Guarding, smarting, snipping intruders away.

When my lover left—well, I had expected as much. I had filled our home with storm and stress. My grief had made him a cuckold.

"Why," he asked me as he packed his bag, "do you light a candle every day in June? Why do your fingertips crackle, why do your lungs sob, why do you ache all night long? Who lashed this woe to your life, and why must I live swaddled in its mien?"

"Go, then," was my only answer. "You have made me no promise. Go and seek more fitting fortune."

For even better measure, I gave him wings to point his way. I watched his skin blister with feathers, his eyes shrink to beads. I watched his face ask the final, desperate *why*; I cackled.

"Because what's mine will never be yours. You can keep the skies. Leave me my earth and the pain that swaddles it. Go and make some swaying branch your home; you'll find no more shelter in mine."

He shrieked, thrusting and snipping with the beak fastened to his once-lovely face. I blocked, I ducked, but I wasn't truly prepared for the venom his love had left behind. He set upon me, wailing, until my left eye ran red and viscous and my right was barely spared.

With that he turned tail and flew. There was no more love in him.

***

I applied all manner of tinctures, of herbs, of muttered

incantations to the bloodied eye, but no use: for the rest of my days it would be milky. A scar-spangled galaxy in my very own face. On the stormier days, I rather liked the effect.

And anyway, even with one eye drained of use, I could see clearer than ever: my precious princess was growing up. Her bones were lengthening; her waist was whittling into womanhood. Time was carving elegance from a chubby child body. I could see her plain as day itself, my womb twinging with every birthday. I marked each one with care, with a mad faith that grew madder still. Soon I'd see what I'd waited for: number sixteen.

***

Do you know what happens to a faery child when her sixteenth year clicks closed? Of course you don't. Mortals never do. They've happened on our secrets, time and again, but the knowledge never lasts. There are things that can't stay in the minds of men, things their thoughts can't quite make room for. As it should be. It's a whole other order. A whole Other.

When a faery child turns sixteen, she puts her childhood to bed.

You say it's brutal. So did I, when I lived among men. I let myself be tamed, if you can call it taming: I see now it was merely a nudging aside. You cannot make a faery other than what she is. What men call brutality is our daily bread. It's simply the way. The world does not spin on an axis of human judgment, whatever they want to think.

When a faery child's youth gives way to the full complement of power, she must prove she can use it. She must prove her prudence, her mercy, her ruth and ruthlessness alike. And it so happens that nature has provided the perfect mark.

On her sixteenth birthday, a faery girl shall kill her father. A faery boy, his mother. Twins share the privilege.

We never birth more than one, not on purpose.

***

*Never bear a mortal's children*, my mother had said. Her fierce face was soft, almost begging.

*The countdown begins from the moment their squalling heads emerge. We are prepared, you and I and the rest of us. We are capable of living the intervening years with grace, even knowing how they will end. A mortal is different. His grief will drive him mad from the child's first cry. He will look at the babe and see only his death, or yours, and he will crumble.*

She took a deep shuddering breath, a half-sob.

*His grief will eat him until he does the job himself. I have seen mortal men slit their own throats, the better to avoid a precious daughter doing the same. I have seen them kill the children themselves. Drown them in the bath and no one is the wiser. I have seen one take the knife to his faery wife's throat, in fury that she lashed him to such a fate. Loving a mortal is pain, my daughter. Kiss him if you must. Tease him and savor that all-too-brief body. But you mustn't take him to your bed.*

I took her words, in my own way. I loved that grandsire, I did. I took him to my bed. But I kept myself barren. Should a seed happen to catch, I snuffed it quick and clean, and put the retching down to a bad cut of fish. He never pushed, and I have always been thankful. He had his wife, after all. His children from a rightful womb. He died having known fatherhood, and every day I am grateful for that. It would have killed me to deny the man anything.

But not his grandson. I could deny that man everything and more.

***

On my daughter's sixteenth birthday, the sun hung red and low, a bloody bulb dripping from the morning firmament.

Aurora's namesake was stirring. I watched the dawn break fiercely, and for the first time and the last, I prayed.

Faeries don't pray. We barter; we don't beg. But on that morning, just for a moment, pride softened in lieu of something tender.

*Let her become herself. That's all I ask. Let the fruits of my womb become what her blood demands, and I will ask nothing more in my lifetime.*

And with that, she knocked upon my door.

I waited before unlatching. I had to fix her in my mind, as though she might fizzle into empty air the moment the hinges creaked. She would shine: curls, curves, and countenance alike. I would know her for mine at a hundred paces. She would be every generation in final, grandest form; she would be what we had waited for. I smelled lightning under her skin, working to a full-bore crackle, and I practically sang.

The knocking rose, a more insistent pitch now. I breathed deeply, my last solitary breath before greeting her precious perfumed presence, and I unlatched the door. It wasn't her.

It was the other mother. The ersatz mother. The other me, gone sixteen years to seed. What was full had turned shrunken; grey converged on buttery blonde. Her eyes were fierce and sad, almost wild. Her dress was splashed with red. She opened her sniveling lips and said:

*Help me. Please.*

Not an apology. Not a *forgive me*. Another beg. A whisper knit with a sob, an echo from all those years ago. I felt my own lip curl.

"This morning I came to my parlor to find--oh, he was white, so white, and drenched in red. And she was leaning over him, her hair trailed all in blood. She looked at me, and I could see it: she *wasn't sorry*."

She was sobbing in earnest now, tears and sweat and spit and blood staining her grey face. How perfectly human. I looked at my Queen, my old striving conniving friend. I let my eye slice away her wrinkles, her sags, her aching mask of a face. Somewhere, she was the girl I had led from squalor to the fripperies of court. When her husband plucked her from the ash and the cinders, his father wept.

*A weed*, he cried. *That girl was born in dirt, and by all that's good and holy she should die in dirt. My son has poisoned his birthright for--what, a slipper? True love--true* lust, *that's all this is, and love of kingdom means nothing! I will die of shame.*

I was the ear. I held the cards. And I liked the girl. She was rough. I liked rough, with or without a diamond underbelly. She was plain and true, she was determined to *win*, and that's what charmed me: she had a touch of the ruthless in her. Clawing out of ashes the way she did, she had to be just a *smidgen* fae.

And I knew love when I saw it. The prince was besotted, a gone man. If I nudged him to happiness, I thought, I'd be that much more comfortable when he ascended the throne himself.

So I put in my word. I stroked, I wheedled, I sweetened the pot here and there. When the knot was tied at last, I greeted the incipient princess in her chambers. I taught her grace and charity. I taught her a proper curtsey. I coaxed her true name, *Eliana*, from her quivering lips. She was titled now, no more *Ella*. I took a bundle of bones and I made a Queen. I loved her like she was mine, and when she brought me her tears, her shame, her knotted womb, of course I did what she asked. Of course. Our race is brutal, but we know what love is.

Now there was blood on her face, there was blood in my memories, there was blood where there used to be ash. There was always a touch of the fae in her. A touch of our brutal, bloody, fiercely loving race. I don't regret what I did next. She had begged at the edges of my world, my womb, my word, until she cracked it open. She had reckoned with faeries and we had finally reckoned back.

I took her hands in mine. "Eliana," I soothed her,

"Ella, sit down."

I coaxed her trembling paleness across my doorstep, and I arranged her in a wooden chair. She sank fleshly into the carved arms and looked at me, full of human gratitude. I turned my back. I bustled at the cupboards. Eliana of the cinders never saw the knife that killed her. It was drawn from my skirts and cozied against her throat before she could cry out. She melted into the assault, her shoulders slackening as they never had in life.

I bent before her to meet her eyes as she bled. I couldn't let her die in middle distance. I took her hand; with my other I steadied her head. She didn't flinch at my milky eye.

"Godmother," she said. "Godmother?"

"Yes, Ella. What is it?"

"Thank you."

***

The cinder queen is buried in the belly of the hearth. I dug deep, deep, deep below my firepit, mounded the dirt until it dwarfed me, and I laid her in. Her husband, the king, my lover's great-great-great, was burned. So I heard. The new vizier, a human of course, had taken one look at the entrails spilling this way and that and given the order. *Torch the evil. No one must know.*

They burned her too, my kingly daughter. The whole village turned up to watch the stake's assembly, the reading of her deeds, the march to the dais where she would meet her grief. I was there, swaddled in somber skirts, my milky eye veiled. No one knew me, not anymore. Least of all my daughter.

But I know she winked, from her bounds against the stake. I know she met my milky eye and smiled, briefly and brightly and meant for no one but me. I know I collected her ashes when my fire was doused. I know they make my hearth burn that much bolder. I know that when the moon is right, my milky eye is almost clear.

## About the Author

Skye Makaris is a writer and antiquarian from Burlington, Vermont. By day she mines the past for truth; by night she takes refuge in fiction. Her literary interests include fairy tales, Puritans, and body horror. She runs the fashion history blog My Kingdom for a Hat; other publications include Body Parts Magazine and Yale's LETTERS Journal.

# IMAGINATION

A. K. SUMMERS

As a child, I always knew I was different. I could see things others couldn't. Some call them ghosts, others call them lost souls, but I once called them friends. I thought seeing them was a gift, but the older I got, I realized it was a burden.

"You have one wild imagination, Emma."

I heard this my whole life. Over and over again my ability was dismissed by so many. I tried to make myself believe that it was just my imagination. I so desperately wanted it to be just that. It was just my imagination. My wild, crazy imagination. My so very real imagination; but, seeing was believing, and this was never my imagination.

It started in the woods. The woods that were home to me. They were my jungle, battlegrounds, fairyland, and any other place I could dream. The trees stretched out far and wide. Some were beautiful, like out of a fairytale, and others were gloomy and had the marks of many years attached to them.

My mom and I had moved here after my parents divorced. She had taken a job that required us to move to a house swallowed up by trees and woodland creatures. I had no friends, except for the ones I found in those woods.

"Emma, you're never going to meet anyone new if you keep making up imaginary friends." My mom used to say all the time.

I was perfectly content with my friends that she couldn't see. With her being an adult, she never believed that my friends were anything other than imaginary. They were always there, climbing the trees with me, laughing and giggling.

I remember the little boy who wore funny looking clothes, tugging on my raven braids telling me to follow him. I can still recall the blue lady, who always brought the cold with her, swimming back and forth in the dirt filled pond.

I liked talking to the man in the cape at night. He

would enter my room and pace back and forth across the hard wood floors. He never spoke, yet I continued to ask night after night what he was doing in my room. I had always hoped that one night he would finally respond, but my mom always interrupted my conversations.

"Your imagination is still working at this time of night? Emma, it's time to put it to bed."

Those were the good old days when the ghosts were known as friends. I didn't realize how quickly that was going to change.

***

New York was supposed to be the perfect opportunity for my mom and me to make it big. She had her own store front now and just enough money to afford a neat little apartment in the Bronx. After living at our house in the woods for eight years, we had moved to an apartment in the city. The plumbing was bad, but the view from the balcony was perfection.

I was getting older and I didn't want to be labeled as a freak. After all, I was the new kid around town and that was bad enough. Being stared at for talking to myself wasn't something I wanted to live with for the rest of my life; so, I decided to let go of my friends.

It was like the spirit world knew that I didn't want to communicate with them anymore. They knew I was the only one who could see and hear them so they continued to try and reach out to me. They would come from near and far and try to ask me questions; but, I pretended I couldn't see them and when I ignored them, they tried harder.

On my 16th birthday, they decided to invite themselves over for the celebration. My cake had flown across the room and my presents were completely destroyed. They did it to get my attention, but I wanted nothing to do with them. I tried to pretend they weren't there, but when my mom saw the disaster she blamed me, I had to tell her.

"It's time to grow up, Emma! Stop blaming your imagination and start taking responsibility for your actions!"

My mom was furious with me. She couldn't take it anymore. She wanted a normal daughter and I couldn't give her that. She blamed me for everything that was wrong in her life.

Between my mother's constant judgment and the voices that broke my sanity, I couldn't do it. As a result of my talking to people that weren't there, the screaming in my sleep because my ghosts and I were no longer friends, my mom decided she couldn't handle it either. She turned to drinking to mute my jabbering and her drinking turned me out of the apartment.

I was on my own with no place to go but on the road with a backpack and my thumb pointed towards the horizons. There was the occasional glance behind me to see if they would follow, but I only saw an empty road stretching for miles. I was sure this time they had left me. I was wrong.

The makeshift hotel along my path loomed over me. The sign that was probably once bright and vivid was now old and faded. It read, "Stargaze Hotel," which was ironic because I wouldn't be caught dead stargazing out here at night.

It was definitely no Hampton, but it was the only hotel who would take what measly cash I had. Walking through the doors I stepped back in time, not the good times. The furniture looked like it had been around since the 60s and the carpet, I was sure, had been there just as long. I didn't know if I was more afraid of ghosts finding me here or a serial killer lurking behind the corners.

My room was not a welcoming sight, the chipping paint and television that just played black and white fuzz was nowhere near inviting. I wanted to turn around and just say, "Keep the money," but I had no place else to go. As my head hit the pillow and my eyes finally shut, the night became more restless than I thought it would be.

My long-lost friends had finally arrived and woke me with knocking on doors, tickling my feet, and turning the faucet off and on. Their shadows played on the walls, mocking my fear. My bed rocked back and forth as my old friends began to whisper to me. My fate was handed to me at that moment. I couldn't escape them. I would simply have to live with it.

***

I got married young, around 20, and I was excited for the new adventure ahead of me. Adam, my husband, and I had bought a home with the picture perfect picket white fence. We planned on starting a family.

The first year marriage is supposed to be bliss, but ours was a nightmare. The ghosts no longer focused on me, but Adam. They didn't want Adam anywhere near me and they would do anything to keep him away. He would wake up with scratches, missing items, and then one day our picture perfect home was burned to the ground. When I told Adam about my burden, he thought I was crazy.

"It's all in your head, Emma. I know you're scared about everything that has happened, but now is not the time to start imagining things," Adam said.

We moved ourselves into a nice little apartment on the top floor of the complex. We fought every day and nothing seemed to get better.

It was during the second week of living there that Adam was mysteriously pushed down the stairs and broke his neck. I knew that they did it, but the authorities thought they knew otherwise. When I tried to explain that I could see what others couldn't, they put me in handcuffs. The last words I remember hearing before I was placed inside the back of the car was, "This woman sure has let her imagination get the best of her."

At almost thirty, I have yet to go crazy. For those of you who would like to differ, I would simply say you, in fact, are the crazy ones. My imagination didn't put me here, though some days I wish it did.

You've all become naïve to what exists and instead of opening up your minds, you've turned your back on it completely. Those out there like you should be locked up, having people pick at your brain to help you see what is real, instead of having people pick your brain to suppress the reality of the darkness that surrounds us.

The pills, which they think numb my mind, simply make it easier for the unknown to become known. They think they are dulling my senses, but I can see them all around me. They are here right now. They are always here. They are standing by my bed, watching me with their unfathomable gaze.

**About the Author**

A.K. Summers has been writing scary short stories since she was a freshman in high school. She knew she had a knack for writing when her teacher said her worked resembled the earlier works of Stephen King. In most of her stories, one can always find the ghosts, vampires, or witches. However, what you won't find are spiders, for she is deathly afraid of them. While she can't pass up the opportunity to write a good fiction story, her true passion resides in film and theatre which is why she is a Creative Writing major, with a concentration in screenwriting, at Southern New Hampshire University. When A.K. has free time, you can probably find her on stage in some community theatre production, or sitting in a corner reading a good book.

# ROT BROTHERS

SIMON McHARDY

It rained this hard only once or twice every summer, Chad and Steven were going to make the most of it. Their greatest joy and terror was riding the creek behind their house on their bodyboards every time it flooded. Their father had told them he didn't want to see them near the creek when it rained; this was all thanks to a story he caught on the evening news about a boy who had been sucked into a drain and drowned. But Chad, at fourteen and two years older than his brother, didn't see the problem, they always bailed out well before the drains. They had sat around all morning waiting for their parents to go shopping, watching raindrops as thick as knitting needles splash on the ground outside and listening to the thunder rolling down from the surrounding hills.

Just before midday they waved their parents off with goodbyes and promises not to go near the swollen creek. The rain was still filling the dry patches in the driveway where the car had been parked when Chad and Steven ran past with their bodyboards and expectant smiles on their faces.

The boys entered the churning waters of the creek at the back of their house, Chad went in first, the water was warm and muddy, bits of debris floated past him, branches, plastic bottles and even a traffic cone.

Steven slid in beside him, "We gonna race?" he said.

"You bet, I'll give you a ten second head start."

"All right you're on, but bet I don't even need it." Steven let go of an overhanging root he was holding and was swiftly carried away in the swirling water. Within a few seconds he was around the bend and out of sight.

Chad saw his brother disappear and pushed off. He grinned madly at the speed with which the water swept him along; the creek had never been this fast before but then he couldn't remember when they had had this much rain. About halfway through the ride he started to get a bit worried, he had glimpsed Steven only twice and each time his brother was just disappearing around the next bend.

He didn't feel like he was making up any ground and he cursed himself for giving Steven a head start. When he turned the last bend, Steven was rushing past the dead elm tree that marked the end of the race.

"Get to the bank," Chad shouted gesturing at his brother who had turned to give him a victorious smirk oblivious to the swiftness of the waters which were torpedoing him to the stormwater drains.

Aware now of the danger Steven began to kick wildly towards the closest bank but the current was too strong and he was whooshed into the sewer, his desperate shrieks rising above the roar of the water. Chad was in the same predicament but at the last minute he was able to grab the edge of the drain where he hung suspended, struggling against the current and screaming his brother's name, the only reply a wet echo.

With no sign of his brother Chad dragged himself to the embankment, trembling from fear and exhaustion. "Dad is going to kill me," he sobbed.

Neither Steven nor his parents were home when he returned. He took a long shower and waited for his parents' arrival.

"Can you help unload the car please, Chad, where's Stevie?" his Mother asked as she piled supermarket grocery bags on to the kitchen table.

"I don't know, Ma, he said he was just going out for walk a while back." His mother looked concerned. Chad gripped his legs with his hands to stop himself from shaking.

"How long ago did he go?"

"About an hour." he tightened his grip, the pain showing in his voice.

"Why did you let him go out in this weather, he's only twelve," his mother glowered at him angrily.

"He didn't want me to go with him."

"I'll go look for him," his father said shrugging into the rain jacket he had just taken off, "he's probably down at the shops playing arcade games."

Chad's parents were in and out all evening taking turns on the phone and driving around the streets looking for Steven. At ten o'clock they called the police who, by late the next day when the rains finally stopped, extended their search to the creek despite Chad's protesting that his brother would not have gone near it. On day two his father found out that Steven's and Chad's boards were missing. Chad insisted that they had lost them last summer and didn't tell him because they didn't want to get in trouble.

***

Steven woke in the wet darkness, he began to move, a bloated and lumbering thing. The pipe had narrowed to the thickness of a man's thigh but his soft, water-logged body moulded into the tight space and he writhed on, worming his way upwards, searching, an entity animated by one need only, vengefulness.

***

A week after Steven's disappearance Chad lay in bed listening to the pipes in his bathroom groan and gurgle, he could go and tell his father but he knew the old man would not appreciate being woken up in the middle of the night for such a thing. He opened the bathroom door and peered down into the dark circle in the sink, some black filth belched out of the hole.

A voice gurgled up from the darkness, "You left me down here to die." Chad jumped back, his eyes bulging in terror.

"Stevie, is that you?" Chad began to inch forward to the sink. A smell of rot wafted up from the hole.

"Have you left any other kids down here to die?"

"Are you trapped, Stevie? I'll go for help." Chad was

peering into sink hole now, almost expecting to see the twinkle of his brother's eye staring up at him.

"Bit late now."

"Why? we can get you out."

"You killed me," Steven roared. Chad fled the bathroom and ran down to his parents' room screaming that he could hear Stevie in the drains. His parents, groggy with sleep, sat up in bed and listened with growing fury and horror as Chad told them about Steven disappearing into the sewer. Armed with this new information the authorities blanketed the sewers. The boys' bodyboards were uncovered but when no trace of Steven was found along the length of the waste water system the night search was called off.

Lying in bed, Chad heard a wet, plopping sound coming from the bathroom, he imagined mincemeat falling on to the floor in small increments. He drew the covers up around him, counting the plops into the thousands before emotionally exhausted he fell asleep.

Towards daybreak Chad woke to a shuffling sound as if something were sliding across the floor of his room, that stink from the bathroom was back but this time it was stronger, he reached for his bedside lamp and flicked it on. He was confused by what he saw, a pink mass of spoiling meat covered the floor like a carpet and crept up the bed and under the covers.

"Come rot with me below, brother."

Chad opened his mouth to scream but the meat enveloped him, flooding the yawning orifice with its decay and gore. The mass slithered back to the bathroom, its prey cocooned and began to squeeze itself through the drain hole, a space the size of a silver dollar. Chad cried out in agony as the bones of his feet snapped like dry kindling, fibula and femur followed, his hips dislocated as he was pulled down, the large bones cracking and splintering noisily. He felt like a boiled lobster living through its own culinary dissection. By the time his ribcage began to snap apart Chad welcomed the mercy of oblivion.

Chad was floating when he regained consciousness, drifting on a stream of shit and piss. The sewer, the dripping reek of it, was all around him. He could hear somebody screaming, it took him a moment to realize that the voice was his, and yet it wasn't, there was someone else screaming with him, inside him, Stevie, they were one now. As they had wormed their way down the pipes together they had merged, Stevie's rotten flesh had melding with his own, a putrid mass of heaving pulp. In the darkness they cursed each other vilely and screamed at the agony of their own putrefaction.

## About the Author

Simon McHardy is an Australian archivist and historian. He has published numerous fantasy and horror short stories which have appeared in such publications as Jitter, Kzine, Devolution Z, Five on the Fifth and 9Tales Told in the Dark. He is currently working on a short story compendium which will be completed in 2018.

# THE TRIALS OF MAN

TEVIS SHKODRA

The nights were bitter and cold. The boy huddled in a grotto's darkness, only a thin cloth garb and some meager red embers of a once-crackling fire to warm his tired bones. Scavengers and predators lurked outside, creeping in the shadows, howling at the moon, drawn to his campfire's flicking light. At night, the boy was forced to sit and shiver in darkness, dousing his flames in fear of an attack. The first raindrops fell early, pattering down on the grotto's steps in front of him. His breath escaped his body in little white wisps of fleeting warmth. His belly grumbled, begging for a meal, clawing at his insides. It promised to be a long night, and when the rains would give way to daylight, he would be forced to hunt again.

He would hunt or he would die.

*Stupid tradition, thought the boy wrapping his arms around his knees. I'm no butcher's son, no smith's boy. My father's not lowborn like them. Why then does he reduce me to their barbaric traditions?*

The world was brimming with talented hunters and skilled warriors, and God knows his father, the king, had coffers spilling with gold. Why then this ritual, this stupid trial of strength?

*A prince should not be forced to hunt when he can pay a lowborn hunter a few silvers for a stag.*

The first two nights, when the hunger seemed to rip his gut open, and the fatigue seeped into his bones, the boy blamed his father. He snuffed his campfire and muttered treasonous insults to the king's health.

With the third night, his head pounded, his muscles weakened, his bones felt brittle, and the boy came to understand. Perhaps it had never been his father's wish. It was the law of the land, of the gods. Even kings were powerless to gods, and gods were powerless to the small folk's rebellious pitchforks.

The entire town knew the prince to be a poor hunter. They saw his stout, chubby frame, padded in layers of fat, his sausage fingers wrapped around his hunting spear. They saw his rosy cheeks and curly red hair, and smiled with a curt bow when he spoke of his upcoming trial.

*This stupid trial is the first law I'm going to change when I become king.*

The next morning when he woke, the ground was moist and tender. The dew was fresh in the air, and the boy emerged from the grotto's mouth with a thirst. He made out to the thick jungles, nimble-footed, silent, and deadly. His spear was heavy to the touch, but its razor-sharp iron tip hungered for flesh.

"A man must provide for his family, just as a king must provide for his people," the boy's father had said. "To the lowborn boys it may be a game, a ritual trial of little value. But you are my son and heir, and our people will soon seek your guidance. How then will they trust you if you have never taken life, never provided for them? You've seen thirteen summers now, and the time has come." His father's tone was like ice. "So leave and return victorious or be banished from our realm forever." The king rested his arms on his son's meaty shoulders and whispering, "I believe in you, son. The gods walk with you."

The prince's farewell was met with silence, with hollow stares. The townsfolk gazed with their dead glances, judged with unsmiling faces, not once curling their lips in a smile or a cheer. The prince had not yet worn the crown and already its weight crippled him. One way or the other, the innocent boy within him would die, from starvation or from duty.

*They must think me dead by now.* The four days since his trial began seemed an eternity. Other boys returned within hours, overnight at most. The lackwitted and sluggish took a little longer. But they were the sons of blacksmiths and hunters, of tailors and fletchers, lowborn peasant boys with wild spirits and savage blood. Four days may as well have been forty. The prince knew nobody would care to look for him. No patrols would comb the woods. No tears would be shed.

*Is Father restless at night, worrying where I am? Does he believe me dead? Has he shed tears for me, or has his disappointment not granted him the courtesy?* These questions haunted the young prince's sleepless nights in the cold, and his long days in the heat. There could be strength in love, he knew, but never love in strength.

His bony hands seemed foreign to him. His fingertips had turned wrinkled and white from the rains. Small rodents skittered by, seeking shelter from the raindrops. Birds perched themselves on treetop branches, peering down on the fat boy-hunter lurking beneath, snapping twigs with his every step.

*The animals can sense me a mile away. They can smell my fear and hear my steps.*

He stared at those plump birds, wanting nothing more than to hurl his spear through the air and watch his dinner plummet down before him. But that was folly. There was no honor in it, no respect for tradition. No, he was not hunting squirrels or rats, birds or even rabbits. It would be unbefitting of a king's son. He was hunting bears, wolves, ferocious jungle beasts that could claw him dead with a single swipe. Had he returned home with anything short of a jaguar pelt around his shoulders, he would have brought shame on his family.

*Would Father remove my banishment if I appear at the city gates holding a plucked goose as my prize?* The thought made him smile. *Perhaps, after four days he will take pity...* But the boy knew that was folly as well. In the king's eyes, death and starvation came second only to honor and tradition. Returning with a small bounty was as good as not returning at all.

Half the morning these fearsome thoughts clouded his muddled mind. The air was silent save for his gut's starving groans. Then came a sharp *snap* from nearby. Something lurked around the corner—a snarling hungry wolf on the prowl, or perhaps a great black grizzly bear?

*Probably just a squirrel,* the young prince assured himself as his hands turned to ice, as his limbs tensed with fear. Armed only with his spear, he crept through the dense trees.

*I am the hunter. The animals should fear me. Not the other way around.*

Then he saw it.

Where the ground depressed into a shallow ravine, at the foot of a thin-flowing stream its pelt seemed to shimmer a rich, hazelnut auburn. How peaceful it looked from afar, a fragile young thing meandering mindlessly in the forest, sipping at the river, perhaps even seeking a small meal of its own. A deer was big game—much bigger than rabbits and squirrels—and peaceful as it was, the boy was famished.

He prowled forward, his eyes fixed on his unsuspecting prey, his bony knees rustling through the tall strands of grass. The deer perked up its ears at the faintest peep, and, after shooting a startled glance left and right, it went right back to sipping from the stream and nibbling at the grass.

*You're a king's son.* His father's words echoed in his mind, their weight falling heavy on the boy's shoulders. *You're a hunter and this is your kill. You're a predator and this is your prey. You're starving and this is your meal. You're cold, and this is your warmth.*

His blood boiled, his heart raced, his mouth watered and his cold hands tingled. The warrior's spirits flowed through him as he prepared to leap for the kill. All the jungle's sounds fell silent, save for his own thumping heartbeat. The boy in him wanted to sit and savor the moment, to approach the gentle beast, run his fingers through its lush pelt. But the other part of him knew the animal must die, if not by his hands today, by another's tomorrow.

In time, everything beautiful met terrible ends, and there was beauty to be found in most everything terrible.

The fabric of time was interwoven in such naturally occurring cycles, of life and death, love and loss, happiness and despair; cycles that had appeared long before the boy's birth and would continue long after his death. It seemed to be a truth hard learned by boys becoming men, a bitter-tasting reality of life widely accepted.

In one fluid motion, the boy leapt up and hurled his spear forward. It *whooshed* through the air, slicing the gentle breeze and piercing the beast's hind. The deer let out a loud, painful groan, followed by a powerful jerk and a whimper. It staggered a few short steps, staining the summer grass behind it with a trail of pooling blood, before finally giving a deep grunt, a soft wail, and collapsing, thudding to the ground.

*I've killed it,* thought the boy, feeling more nauseous than proud, his craven little heart sinking with fear.

He approached with slow, careful steps, noticing the fear in the animal's wide, black eyes. Its body was still warm to the touch. Its heart still pounded softly, chest puffing up and down as it drew out slow, hot breaths. The deer jerked and moaned when the boy ran his fingers through its pelt, its eyes widening with fear.

Half of the boy rejoiced for the meal he was about to enjoy, while the other half wept for the life he was about to take. He had once thought a prince should never be privy to the world's injustices. Yet, stroking the dying animal's pelt, the boy realized the good and the evil would always be twined together, one white and the other black, mingling to form the endless gray expanse they inhabited.

*Is this what Father means to teach me? Does he want his son a killer, to bear the burden of my actions? Is savagery necessary to manhood? If so, I'll have no part in it.* But his hunger scraped his insides. The animal was far too heavy to carry back into town. Its blood was almost black as it pooled around the boy's knees. In one fluid motion, the boy jerked the spear from the animal's hind and brought it down on its chest. The soft white underside of its belly stained with blood as the beast's eyes widened.

The boy made camp at the thin stream's basin, under an oak's shade. He stripped from the dear what he needed, a tender cutlet to cook over the campfire, and a stained fur pelt to warm his night.

The butchers had told him when he was younger that an animal's fear spoils its meat. It was true. The cutlets tasted of ash. The foul stench of blood and death swirled in the boy's nostrils as he wrapped the still-hot, fleshy pelt around his shoulders. The flies and the scavengers soon gathered, attracted by death and fire, to consume the carcass the boy had left behind. The flames glistened in the deer's hollow black eyes, which stared blankly at the young prince.

On that fourth night, he ate like a king, almost gnawing off his fingers in the meal's frenzy. Then he slept better than he had in days, with a soft pelt around his shoulders, a bellyful of meat, and a crackling fire at his feet. Waking up the next morning, it seemed like a dream.

When the sun had risen, the dead beast still lay there mangled and skinned, an odorous stench hovering in the air. A few of the braver scavengers, vultures and rodents, pecked at the raw, fleshy bounty. Others lurked in trees and in bushes, their yellow eyes poking though the shade, waiting. The boy's conscious began to torment him that morning, but only when his hunger was sated, after the deed was done.

His trial was over, his banishment lifted. He sought nothing more than to leave this savage jungle running, and return home a man.

*It was Father's will, and Father's will is law. Do all boys feel this way their first time—strange and tingling all over, ashamed and dirty, but also oddly satisfied?*

Specks of deer's blood had dried black on his shoulders and face, forming a thin mud-like layer of filth. His white garb was smudged with streaks of crimson. The animal's pelt itched the boy's neck, resting askew and uncomfortable on his shoulders. But he wore it proudly upon his return home, perking his meaty shoulders up to keep the thick pelt from slipping off.

*What will the townsfolk think—to see their prince returning spear in hand, bloodstained, and wearing the skin of his prey? Will they greet me a warrior, or some lowborn brute? Will they smile and clap or will they shy away, repulsed? Will they see me still the same frightened boy, or a man worthy of their respect?*

The questions kept his mind racing.

Approaching familiar lands, his chest tightened from an anxious fear, his insides churned, his hands became clammy with sweat, and his jaw clenched.

Thin fingers of black smoke rose in the distance, above the tree line and over the small ridges of land.

*There it is. There's home.*

The delicious and familiar smells seemed to already waft to his nose. Perhaps the king would throw a banquet feast to celebrate his son's triumphant return, perhaps a celebration for the small folk.

With the ridge behind him, and the town approaching, the boy caught a glimpse of the road ahead, lonely and abandoned.

*Where's the town guard? Where are the villagers plowing the fields?*

The thin fingers of black smoke, he soon after realized, rose from burning homes, laid to siege from tall red flames. His heart sank at the sight. The town's stonewalls had crumbled to ruin, the homes they had once protected were plundered and scorched to the ground, the citizens slaughtered by the hundreds. The survivors, few as they were, must have sought shelter into the woods, or perhaps were made prisoners.

Dead bodies surrounded the young prince as he walked down familiar neighborhood paths. Strangers' hollow faces frozen in the terror of the moment, their cheeks sunken, and their eyes red and tearstained with grief. The faces of his friends and neighbors looked up at him with their haunting dead eyes. Only the vultures rejoiced, feeding aplenty on the mounds of human fodder. Flies buzzed about, and with them, the stench of death.

Only a few survivors remained in the black rubble, none caring to see the prince's return. They did not so much as glance in his direction. Once, perhaps, there may have been kings and princes ruling over their domain, but when the city had fallen so had their loyalties and homes. The handful yet living were frail and skinny, waifs with bare goose fleshed legs, blackened from the charred remains of their homes, donned in nothing but torn rags, wandering aimlessly, scavenging alongside the vultures.

The young prince stood over the rubble that was once his kingdom, and wept. He wept for his father, for the man's legacy, for his friends and kin, for his home, for his past and future. He wept for his trial, his banishment, for having been forsaken to a hunter's life, a bandit's life, a savage life in the company of beasts. He wept for his childhood buried under the rubble of those buildings, and for the countless perils life would soon spring upon him.

## About the Author

Tevis Shkodra is a recent university graduate and short story writer living in Toronto, Ontario. He always seems to have one-too-many projects on his plate, whether that is an edgy new short story, or an idea-turned-novel in the works. When he's not writing, he's carving out time for painting or curling up in bed with the classics.

# THE WALL'S END

RUDOLFO A. SERNA

It was a hulking wall, a giant spine, half-buried in the desert sand.

Dust from the asteroid's collision had encircled the planet. Blinding and suffocating, the sands never stopped washing over the wall's ruins that pierced twilight and dawn in an auriferous sky that the moon had taken into its swollen arms. The moon loomed half-broken and crumbled, anchored among belts of debris formed from the meteor's impact.

The wall was too high to pass, and the caravan of Pilgrims that wandered its length wore the goggles, air masks, and cloaks that protected them against the sandstorm. They followed the carriages pulled by the modified camelus that were smaller than their extinct predecessors, bred for food and burden, designed to last longer and breed faster, as were the Pilgrims who had been modified in the laboratories of the Engineers' cave. The yelping animals pulled the carriages, made of wood and rotted canvas, pans chiming against the wooden frames. Inside one of the carriages, a dying infant slumbered, tucked in blankets.

The caravan stopped beside the massive wall, and the sentries set up their watch for the night, digging in the sand for protection against the winds or attackers, while the others stretched out their canopies against the megalith. Cinched, the canopies snapped with each gust that pulled at the knots and fasteners.

The camelus, staked to poles in the sand, knelt and nuzzled their snouts into each other's musky flanks looking for comfort.

In dull lamp light, Mesah dropped back the hood of her cloak and removed the goggles, her eyes glowing the same dull orange light as that of the lamp. She leaned over her child and placed her hand on the infant's feverish brow, taking a small silver box from under the bundle of blankets she opened it.

The vial of green solution gave off a faint glow. Mesah

broke the seal and drew the green serum into a syringe and injected her baby, hoping that this one injection would keep her from having to sever the child's head.

Mesah felt Salem breathing behind her in the dark while she hovered over their child with the empty syringe.

"He will live," Mesah said.

Salem looked at the infant struggling to breathe.

"It will save him," she said.

"It's not the infection that is killing him," Salem said. "He is immune."

"Then why is he sick?" Mesah said. "The Engineers did not finish the experiments."

"The world is ..."

"He will live," she said.

"Without modification?"

"He will live," she insisted.

"You shouldn't have given it to him," Salem said.

It was the only sample of the antidote that had been created too late to save the old race from the global pandemic.

Scientists had engineered the cure hoping that the Pilgrims would deliver it to those who were still trapped in the monastery bunkers. The Pilgrims had barely escaped the caves, and when they reached the wall, they were unable to cross over or go back--all they could do was follow it.

Mesah gave their dying child the last of the antidote, not caring about the dying old world or the new one coming into being.

The new world had begun under streaks of falling lunar rock and bits of the shattered, cratered moon, that seemed close enough to touch. The debris orbited just at the edge of the atmosphere, falling and exploding in the orange night sky.

From the hole dug out of the sand, the sentries scanned the desert, the glow in their eyes brightening and dimming with the light from the moon.

Recognizing the temperature signatures of the lumbering Humans through their ocular implants, the Humans' spectrums registered cold. They grabbed the handles of the blades fashioned from broken-down machines they'd encountered abandoned along the wall, the occupants long gone.

Through blowing sand, the Humans staggered towards the camp, burnt by wind and particle, skin dry and paper-thin, driven by hunger.

Mesah and Salem heard the sentries' shouts.

Mesah swept the child into her arms, strapped him to a carrier, placed it on her back and stepped outside to the glaring moonlight. Salem stepped out beside her, then, hearing the frantic bleating of the camelus, he ran towards the sounds of the sentries calling.

The Pilgrims' battle cries mixed with the wind and groans of the camelus. From her position outside the tent, Mesah saw, under the bright crumbling moon that crossed the high rim of the ruins, a group of Humans emerge from the haze.

Mesah pulled free one of the coiled ropes from the side of the carriage and unraveled it. She took the grappling hook and swung it with all of her strength to the top of the wall. Desperately she hoped that the metal barbs would catch hold, but instead the hook bounced off the side of the wall.

She pulled the gaff from the ground and swung it again. Its tip scraped the surface before it cratered in the sand next to her.

The Humans lurched towards her.

Mesah threw the grappling hook one last time with all of her strength, and watched the tip take hold in some unseen crack high above in the darkness.

She started to pull herself up the wall, feeling the strain in her arms, the heels of her boots against the rough concrete face of the monolith as she reached up, feeling the straps of the pack digging into her shoulders with her dying child as she pulled. Getting away from the hands of the snarling Humans that reached up for them. She pulled herself further out of their reach. She could see the rotted-out eye sockets of the faces burnt by the sand and wind, their clothes long ago shredded from their skeletal frames, exposing the bellies of the terminally starved.

She pulled harder with her arms that had been modified for greater strength, and dangled above the ravaged Humans, suddenly unaware of her child crying or the Humans bellowing beneath her, as she felt the grapnel breaking loose of its hold...

She plummeted into the waiting hands, the long dagger-like nails and the black teeth. She felt their bony fingers grasping at her and the child.

Salem was jamming his blade down through one Human head after another, and beating them off the camelus, when he heard Mesah scream. He looked back toward the tent where he had left Mesah and the child.

Humans were swarming over her and the baby, trying to get at the meat. They bit into her arms and scratched at her face. They piled on top of her and blocked out the moonlight. All was going pitch black. Mesah's eyes stopped glowing, and she screamed louder, realizing that her child was still beneath her, but she couldn't move with the weight of them on her chest, and the stench of desiccated flesh everywhere.

Salem and the others ran towards Mesah and the pack of Humans on top of her. The Pilgrims pulled the Humans' heads back, slashed their necks, left the heads dangling sideways by strips of skin. The empty sockets opened and closed; the mouths kept gnawing at empty space, still hoping to feed.

They pulled the Humans off Mesah and the child, but it was too late. The crying had stopped. The child had been crushed under his own mother's weight.

They pulled her bloody body up from the ground, she could still feel him on her back. She stared at the wall. The long giant casting its shadow, the pieces of moon sparking and disintegrating as they skittered across the edge of the planet's atmosphere.

The child looked unharmed, except for a scratch across its face. *A possible point of infection,* Salem thought. He could see the temperature of the body already cooling. He expected the tiny body to rise, even though it shouldn't. Even if it hadn't been modified to resist the inhospitable conditions of their world, it was still their offspring. It was born immune, and would not rise from the dead. Salem knew that the antidote would not have the effect Mesah had hoped, and that it could only be given to those that had the mutative gene. The child did not move. It would remain dead, he thought, thanks be to their makers, the Engineers.

Mesah began wailing a tortuous sound.

Salem was afraid that it would bring more of the Humans, but the winds picked up and her crying echoed against the wall, and after a while it just sounded like the wind.

Samson, Salem's younger brother, sat out in the dunes with his hood up over his head, watching the camp and the spine of the wall snake across the desert, his eyes glowing with the moon. "The baby, the baby," he kept saying to himself.

***

In the orange daylight, Salem surveyed the wall.

A hill of rubble rose above the Pilgrims, and above the rubble, the moon, poised bright, close enough, it seemed, that they could climb to its broken surface. It hovered over them, but soon the illusion of proximity dissipated, and the ring of debris that entered the atmosphere began glittering.

Mesah slept in the carriage, she was designed to heal quickly from her wounds. Like the other Pilgrims, she was immune to the infection, and the bite and scratch marks were already closing. But the child had died in the fall, and Mesah would not be able to heal from his death as easily.

Crying in her sleep, Mesah fell again into the putrefied hands reaching for her, the infant still strapped to her back, the moment made vivid by the implants that replayed the image again and again, driven by trauma in a kind of psychic high-def.

The Engineers' science had worked after all, Salem had thought--there was no resurrection of the flesh. Salem had hoped to preserve the corpse, to keep the antidote inside the child, to make of his body a kind of vessel to be delivered to someone who could extract it.

Salem could neither weep nor mourn for the child; his programming did not allow it.

The child had been wrapped in blankets and separated from his mother. The body would have to be prepared and mummified, rewrapped in burlap and carried with them to the sea.

Salem climbed the rubble to the first breach they had found since walking the length of the great wall, hoping to find a place where they could cross to the other side, maybe even find something green—a tree, some grass—but all he saw were sandstorms to the horizon, and he realized that there was only more desolation on the other side.

"Salem, what do you see?" his little brother Samson called out hopefully from the foot of the rubble.

"Nothing!" Salem called back.

"Nothing? Nothing?" Samson crawled up the ruins.

"There's nothing," Salem said, rubbing dust from his eyes.

"Nothing," Samson said. "Nothing. Climb and climb, but we never find what we need."

"No. We don't, it seems." Salem placed his hand on the young Pilgrim's head as he passed him on the way back down.

"The ocean is wet, sad and sweet, green," Samson said.

"It will cool our feet." His shoulders began shaking. "It will cool our feet, brother. I cry..."

"Yes. Cry, Samson. Go ahead."

Salem left his brother sobbing and made his way to the base of the wall.

The other Pilgrims gathered, dressed in their tattered cloaks. When they removed their goggles and air masks, they resembled what the Humans once looked like, before the modifications made them preternaturally strong with eyes that glowed at night.

The ridges on the other side of the vast crater could not be seen in the blowing sand, and the rest of the wall that had once crossed the continent disappeared in a red haze of blowing dirt from the crater.

The Pilgrims donned their air masks and goggles, and Samson climbed down from the rubble. It was as if the others did not want to see the desert world they had inherited. They lined up to descend into the giant crater gouged out by what could only be a part of a falling moon, an asteroid, or missile, set loose by one government or the other that shared the border. Desperate to stop the walking plague, and break open the surface of the earth, and shatter the desert and a section of the giant wall that traversed the landscape.

They would have to find a way to the other side of the deep crevasse, to cross the crater to find the other end to the wall's ruins which they could then follow to the ocean.

They watched for anything that moved in the red haze below them.

The animals were herded down a steep slope. The animals had been designed for such conditions, but they could only last so long without food or water, and the feed pellets were running low, as were the near empty canisters of water they carried.

They would all starve.

They had lost three from the herd to the Humans that had jumped on the animals' backs, grabbing their legs, bringing them down, crawling over them, biting and slashing, until the camelus bled to death, while being eaten. A fourth one was barely saved, but strong enough to keep up with the rest of the herd, healing quickly.

The Pilgrims would need the herd to survive, or they would all eventually perish, to be eaten by the old race or covered by the desert sand.

At the bottom of the immense canyon size crater they were protected from the winds. They stopped to rest in the red dust, but one of the pack animals got loose and wandered away from the rest of the herd, running free into the red haze among the rocks.

The shepherd chased after it, following its tracks into a crevice that was just wide enough for the animal to fit through.

The shepherd followed. Slipping through the crack, she could see the camelus's tail, and then its head reaching up and biting into the tentacles that protruded from a purplish, faceless, malformed body attached to the end of a long fleshy green stalk that sprouted from the stone and red soil.

The shepherd continued to stare at the aberrant life forms that covered the crater floor, the languid sway of the fish skinned tendrils that grew from the purple torsos, the tops moving in waves, the gleaming skin changing colors, and the shepherd almost didn't notice the cold water soaking though her weathered boots.

***

Salem heard the voices of the other Pilgrims who had followed the shepherd through the break in the crater.

When he arrived, he found them reaching out to the tentacles that flickered with translucence. Salem could not recognize the life form, nor did he recall seeing them depicted in the old books he had studied.

The tentacle forest fluctuated between purple and

green, shimmering in the orange light, and it was unclear to Salem whether they were plants or animals.

But the shimmering of their flesh did not deter the Pilgrims, who dropped on their stomachs and plunged their faces into the shallow stream flowing from somewhere beyond the morphon garden.

The starving pilgrims began ripping pieces of flesh from the creatures' limbs, stuffing it into their mouths.

A soft crying began to echo through the narrow gorge.

Salem panicked, thinking it were Humans moaning from somewhere nearby, but then he realized that the sound was different, high and melodic, like a song he had heard from old recordings of a choir not Human at all, but angelic. The sound seemed to be coming from the glimmering creatures.

Salem pulled some spongy flesh from a tentacle and felt the minute hairs. He bit down lightly on the velvety surface, hoping that his modified digestive tract would process the organism should it be poison.

Salem chewed the bitter flesh. When he swallowed, he could feel the tiny hairs going down his throat. He reached down to the clear flowing water at his feet, cupped a handful and drank. He could feel the grit, but the water was clean, and it did not have the stale metallic taste of the canisters.

The other Pilgrims fed and splashed water on their faces, laughing and acting as if there were no more roving Humans to threaten them. They ignored, too, the cries of the creatures they ate alive.

Salem dug a piece of flesh from the purplish limb of one of the morphons to carry back to Mesah as an offering to his mate who had been chosen for him.

He turned to leave, but through the haze, he saw a large black stone embedded in the red rock of the crater wall, the onyx stone's surface pockmarked with shimmering purple and blue crystallinity. And like the purplish green bodies that the Pilgrims ate, the black crystalliferous stone was, to Salem, of an unknown origin.

He was surprised to see Mesah through the haze.

Her arms were bandaged and she was carrying the corpse of their child, still wrapped in a blanket, towards the wailing garden.

"Mesah!" Salem called, but she walked past him and laid the body of their child on the rocks at the foot of the alien field that swayed and wept under the bright moon and orange sky.

She knelt before the creatures.

"Save him!" she begged. "I know you can. Save him!"

The rest of the Pilgrims stopped plucking at the purple-green stalks, stopped drinking the water from the trickling stone.

Salem watched Mesah kneel.

Slowly, one by one, the rest of the Pilgrims began to kneel before the wailing beings. These were children of the new age, not Human, something more, yet still they prayed and believed in the supernatural.

"Save him!" they said, their voices merging with the cries of the morphon. "Save him!"

Salem watched the Pilgrims wishing the infant would live again, to smile and laugh as children were meant to.

Salem and the others had been designed by the Engineers to replace the old race, but it was not known whether their offspring would survive without further modification.

"*Save him.*" The words almost sprang from Salem's mouth, but he resisted. He knew that the infant would not return, that the Engineers' science would keep the child from wanting to return and destroy them.

Though it carried the antidote within its body, the child had been too weak to survive. It had not been modified to exist in the new world. *Maybe if they had more time to grow him, make him stronger*, Salem thought.

"Save him," the Pilgrims continued to chant, "save him," and Salem continued to feel the urge to say the words, but he did not.

Mesah picked up the child and felt the bundle in her arms move.

Her eyes glowed with the moonlight. She looked down at him.

"See! I knew you could save him!" she cried to the tentacled creatures. Their tendrils rose up to the clouds that sparkled with lunar debris.

The infant had worked itself free from the blanket.

Mesah held him and put him to her breast to nurse.

His cold lips broke the skin, drawing blood that mixed with her breast milk, yet she still cuddled the child, fed him, the wet sounds gurgling up from his throat.

Behind Salem, Samson began to sob and mumble to himself, "sad and sweet, sad and sweet." He shook his head and sobbed, his eyes beginning to glow. "They were wrong, Salem, they were wrong..."

The Engineers and their science had failed. More modifications were needed.

The wailing garden continued singing its angelic song, the moon rained down over the ruins of the last world, and the Pilgrims found out that they were all too Human still.

Salem reached for his blade.

## About the Author

Rudolfo A. Serna has a penchant for 70's horror B-movies, psychedelic doom metal, permaculture, and nature worship. A native of northern New Mexico, his previous occupations have included carpenter, landscaper, wildland firefighter, and adjunct professor. He lives with his wife and daughter in Albuquerque, NM, writing dark fantasy sci-fi. His short stories can be seen with Brick Moon Fiction and Bewildering Stories. He earned an MFA in Creative Writing from the University of New Mexico, and he is the creator and digital steward of the Mutantroot Art Collective.

More of his work can be found at:
www.mutantroot.com/rudolfo-serna

# THE FORGOTTEN HOUSE

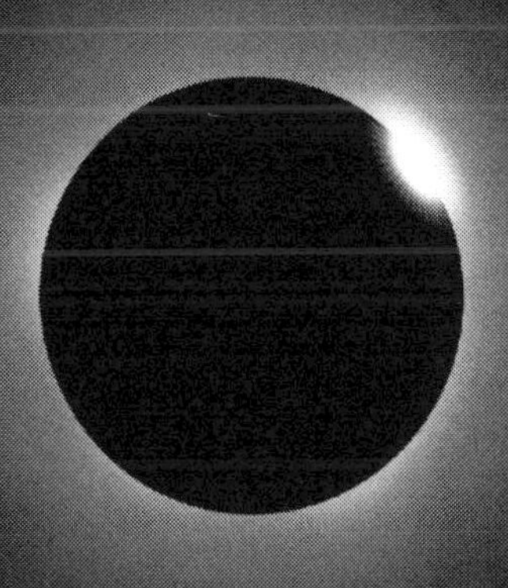

S. J. BUDD

Monday morning passed slowly on the 8:02 south-eastern train into London; Kirsten willed it so. *Please not yet*, she begged, *how I hate that place.* But still the train pushed on with its sombre cargo of dejected people destined for another week of work in grey offices with grey faces and conversation. The train weaved through pretty cultivated suburbs like a cavalcade of dread, a cold thought pressing through into an otherwise happy mind.

Kirsten looked around at the empty faces sunk deep in their phones and tablets. Instead of taking their cue she entertained her heart, which was a hungry hunter; always needing more. She watched the houses pass by as she lost herself in a daydream wondering about the sorts of people who lived in those houses. She dreamed about the sort of house she would like to end up in one day when he search for the *one* was over. She would find somewhere, along a train line and make it into a real home. A home that people would look from the train and wished they lived in it. One by one the houses briefly opened up and allowing Kirsten a brief glimpse inside as the train shuttled through. Her shoulders slumped slightly. Why was she always on the outside looking in?

There was one house that always caught Kirsten's imagination. It stood out against its handsome neighbours, which had all been modified and improved with extensions and conservatories. It seemed forgotten and abandoned by everyone else, and because of that Kirsten felt a strange affinity to it. For she too had been forgotten.

Just by looking at it from the back Kirsten could tell it belonged to a desirable street full of happy fulfilled families. But this house seemed darker than the others. Its large savage garden had been left to grow as it desired, without human intervention. Piles of bricks and debris piled up against the rickety wooden fence that leaned to one side. It's not somewhere one would want to live but the home possessed something the others homes did not; unrealised potential. There was something about that house that drew her in.

Kirsten moved closer to the window. She sat in the same seat each day so she could do this. The train began its slow descent to the next station. She felt the breaks choke the speed as it began to slow. Soon the house would be visible. She waited for it to appear. One day she would buy that house and turn it into a beautiful home. That was the one she wanted.

Her eyes opened wider. The house, which seemed so devoid, finally offered up a clue. Standing in the garden was a person hidden away in an oversized grey hoodie hanging low over their face. It appeared to be a workman, their clothes were heavily stained and worn. All perfectly normal but yet there was something amiss with the way the figure stood. Feet far apart standing proud and free as if inviting people to stare and behold what it was they exhibited in their outstretched hand.

The figure stared right back at Kirsten, she knew that despite not being able to see their face. It was more accurate to say she felt them staring back, two pairs of eyes making an unseen yet felt connection. The stranger's head titled as if in asking a silent question as Kirsten's eyes slowly moved over to what they held.

She gasped and looked around at her fellow passengers who uniformly sat motionless looking down too absorbed with the phones and devices in their hands. *Surely I'm mistaken…*

To make matters clearer for her the figure moved forwards slightly holding up their bounty higher for her to see. She flinched away burrowing up against the large man next to her. Still he did not look up out of the window. Her brain worked in a frenzy trying to reject what her eyes saw. That it wasn't a human head in the person's hand. Judging by the rich red dripping down it was fresh. The deceased eyes were still open and turned up to the sky in weary resignation. The mouth hung open in terror, frozen with death in mid scream.

"Someone, anyone, look," Kirsten implored to the carriage of people before realised each pair of ears were plugged up with headphones. Tinny music came from their phones as she urged herself to look away. The train pulled into the next station, people got off and more people got on.

Tuesday morning came with trepidation. Kirsten looked down playing with her hands and scratched her arms until they were red. All night she had debated calling the police but each time she went to dial she hung up. Something stopped her. Surely someone else on her train would have seen and called the police? She also couldn't ignore the strange feeling that someone had the home she wanted, that somehow she was jealous. She wanted to be the one to make it beautiful. She wanted that house badly.

Kirsten always sat in the same seat in the same carriage. She did again today. She had considered sitting somewhere else that morning. Somewhere on the other side so that she couldn't be seen from the window but it would have meant that she would have to sacrifice her view of looking out.

Once more the train began to slow as it prepared itself for the next station of human cargo. The morning was grey with London smog hung heavy with mist. Inside the train the windows were glazed with human breath. Quickly she moved her hands to wipe clean the window as the train came to pass by the house that had been forgotten.

She felt that strangeness again. This time there was no severed head but the figure still stood there. Standing in the same spot with feet wide apart. This time accompanied with a worktable and saw. Since yesterday there had been a noticeable amount of work being undertaken in the gloomy house.

It seemed like the kitchen had been ripped out and all the windows had been opened. She clenched her fists unable to do anything but watch.

Within her mind there was a click. The stranger turned

around to face Kirsten in greeting. Again the hand outstretched and it pointed right at her, she felt its clutching at her chest as if trying to pull her free from the train as it meddled through. Kirsten cried out grabbing at the man next to her who did not look up as he shrugged her off and got back to his paper.

All day at worked Kirsten chastised herself for having an over active imagination. Once more her hand reached for her phone to dial 999 before abruptly taking it away. She was being silly, things like this didn't happen to people like her. She must have been mistaken. As she lay awake at night she vowed that if anything seemed amiss the next morning she would call the police.

Wednesday came with the calm after a maelstrom of worry. She knew it was in her head. That she was being silly. Before getting aboard she had picked up one of the free newspapers and read avidly deciding to ignore everything that was going on around her. Trying to become like the others on the train.

However when the time came, when the train began to slow she knew she would have to look up. She had promised herself she wouldn't. That she wouldn't allow this stranger to tease and scare her any more. She pulled her handbag closer to her, which was weighed down by a hammer hidden inside.

Yet when she looked out there was no one there. The garden was empty and all the windows stood shut. There was a calmness around the house. It was no longer the pitiful property that she had long since admired. Now the house seemed ready for her with new curtains in place, a fresh coat of paint and colourful flowers beading the flowerbeds in the back garden. The house passed from view and Kirsten sighed smiled and shook her head. Excitement was running through her. Only two more days until the weekend. Now she felt stupid for bringing a hammer into work with her.

Kirsten turned the page of her paper. A shiver ran

through her as she felt a click. Directly opposite her fellow commuter slowly lowered their paper revealing an oversized grey hoodie and heavily stained work trousers.

Underneath their pulled down hoodie which concealed their face in shadow came three cold words, "It is ready."

## About the Author

Originally born in Cornwall, south west England, her childhood was surrounded by myths and legends. She has always been fascinated by anything out of the ordinary. It was in this strange and ancient land where she developed a passion for writing.

Her work has appeared in over twenty magazines including Sanitarium Magazine, Siren's Call Publications, Deadman's Tome, Aphotic Realm, Aphelion, Bewildering Stories and Blood Moon Rising Magazine.

Twitter @sjbuddj

Her debut collection of short stories, *Spells and Persuasions*, is out now on Amazon.

# PERSISTENCE OF MEMORIES

JOHN N. CRAIN

A warm mist descended over the crèche and K raised its head above the polished stone rim. Not much to see, but the moisture made odors stronger. K opened an olfactory port, analyzing the heady mix of scents, some sweet, some bitter, some so strong they could be tasted. Woven through the tapestry of redolence, K detected something new, a thread of effluvium never encountered. K's primary pseudopod flowed over the side of the nest, following the strange aroma, seeking the source.

***

On bare knees, Miyoko knelt over a portable atmospheric sensor. She worked naked in the alien environment, pleasant beyond their expectations, warm, humid, pervaded by an unearthly fragrance she rather liked. She and her fellow crewmember, Winston, had decided to dispense with their cumbersome suits as soon as they'd landed.

Her sole margin of safety was the narrow strip of metallic plastic, her Guardian, clinging to her right forearm like a synthetic skin. Winston was always tinkering with it, improving it, and its versatility still astounded her though she'd almost ceased to notice it. Other implanted strings, less obvious, more a part of her, aided her thought processes, regulated her physical being down to her cellular structure.

She adjusted the sensor a slight degree. The glowing telltale changed from orange-brown to a pleasing green and she knew its results could be trusted. As she rose and turned to go back to the ship, something touched her ankle.

***

Stretched out in his berth, Winston allowed his thoughts to be lulled by the hum of eleven-dimensional strings working in unison, a subatomic symphony created by the Witten Device. The instruments producing that sound enabled instantaneous travel to any point in the universe; the underlying technology had superseded electronics more than a century ago when Winston was just a boy. Strings ruled human existence now.

He and Miyoko found the planet three days ago, after bouncing around this neighborhood of the galaxy in what might have appeared to be a random fashion for the better part of a week. But it wasn't random. With each hop, subsequent surveys added more details about the sub-quadrant until a set of coordinates came up blue-green, indicating a planet capable of supporting human life. Their craft duly popped into existence a few hundred miles above the surface. Sensing and cataloguing began.

Such a benign planet. Life in abundance, none of it too threatening. Water too, of course – the atmosphere just seemed like an extension of the countless bodies of fresh water. No oceans or significant mountains – from orbit the planet most resembled a huge, spherical sponge.

Winston's ruminations ended abruptly when he heard a scream, somewhat muted by the thick, moist atmosphere outside the ship's open hatch. In his haste, he came close to slipping on the dewy metal threshold, but regained his balance and ran in the direction where he and Miyoko previously agreed to set up the sensor.

He rounded a boulder, almost stumbling over Miyoko where she lay on the ground, face contorted in pain. An electric blue aura encased her entire body. Her Guardian had automatically activated a shield the instant it sensed distress. Miyoko's hand gripped her left calf above the ankle, fingers causing the adjacent skin to appear much whiter than usual. At first, Winston thought she'd sprained her ankle somehow, and wondered how such a minor injury could be so painful, but when he bent over it he understood. An oblong hole not much larger than a finger marred the flesh. With great care he rotated her leg to get a better look. Very little blood, yet the wound extended half an inch deep, revealing bone. The pain would be excruciating and he was amazed she hadn't passed out. Bewildered, he raised his eyes to hers, questioning. "What happened?"

"Something attacked me. No warning– otherwise my Guardian would've kick in. I didn't get a good look at it – it was too fast – behind those rocks." She pointed beyond the sensor unit, ten feet away, toward a small rock formation covered with patches of the ubiquitous vegetative growth resembling lichen.

Winston edged around the formation and his own Guardian, sensing his wariness, put up a tentative shield that could be reinforced in an instant should the need arise. A prickling sensation emanated from the Guardian and traveled up his forearm indicating preparedness of becoming a weapon. A creature the size of an average dog lay on the ground. Winston froze, observing the thing. Though it didn't seem to be going anywhere, it wasn't motionless either. It possessed no definable shape, constantly shifting, flowing from one amorphous configuration to another. Winston's fascination grew and he realized the creature's movements were oddly calming. The prickling in his arm subsided and he stepped forward. A portion of the mutating mass formed what might have been described as a head, but featureless except for several round, flat spots Winston supposed fulfilled the function of eyes, for they arranged themselves on the changing surface as though they looked at him. And indeed, an immediate reaction ensued that Winston interpreted as fear. The creature backed away, quivering.

Winston squatted, studying the creature. The quivering ceased. Though the creature's mass didn't appear to be supported by any skeletal structure, it wasn't as formless as he'd initially thought. The head-like portion expanded and contracted, as did other parts of the creature. An almost cylindrical, tapering appendage began to form on the surface of the creature closest to Winston, stretching outward, and Winston became vaguely alarmed again, causing his shield to brighten and a renewed prickling along his arm. But as he started to stand, the rubbery appendage curled like the trunk of an elephant, touching the ground. Though he couldn't say why, Winston received the distinct impression that the gesture was non-threatening, perhaps even a gesture of peace.

Winston's fascination with the creature broke, interrupted by a sudden concern for Miyoko, still in pain. He turned to retrace his steps, keeping an eye on the creature. As he moved away, it followed, maintaining a benign distance. As Winston reached Miyoko, the creature came into her view. Her eyes widened but she retained her composure, governed by her scientific training. In an even tone she said, "That's what injured my leg. Don't let it touch you."

"I don't think it meant to hurt you. How's the pain?"

"My Guardian has it under control now. I think I could walk without much trouble."

"Good. Let's get you back to the ship."

He helped her up – damp, flawless skin slipping against skin – and she kept her gaze on the creature, which had stopped moving toward them, as though waiting. She took one tentative step, verifying the absence of any significant pain, let go of Winston's arm and continued in the direction of the ship. The creature resumed its undulating motion and followed.

***

Winston gazed out the ship's hatch at the creature twenty paces beyond. It gazed back at him, or seemed to with its unreadable disk-like eyes, and he considered the old adage that the eyes are the windows to the soul. Winston didn't believe in the concept of soul. He turned to find Miyoko already in the care unit. She winced for the brief moment her Guardian relinquished pain management and the more capable care unit took over. New flesh began filling the hole in her leg. In less than a minute the repair was complete and Miyoko stepped out of the unit, reached down and rubbed the spot where the injury had been. "Still just a tiny bit sore," she commented.

"I'm sure it won't be for long."

"Thanks for coming to my rescue. I'm sorry I screamed, but the pain was so sharp and unexpected I couldn't help it."

Winston shrugged. "That creature – it's not at all like the others we've seen on this planet, every one of them harmless – I thought we'd catalogued them all."

"This one seems so different. Smaller, no apparent bone structure to support it. I wonder how such an organism could have evolved on this planet… It's very interesting, don't you think?"

He gathered her into his arms and marveled at her resilience. "Yes, extremely. It seems to have more advanced cognition than anything else we've found here."

"What makes you think that?"

"Nothing specific – just a feeling… Even though it doesn't have a definable shape, it seems to use a kind of body language..."

"Winston, I think we should start our rest period early. I'm sure the stress affected you too. We could use the common berth if you like…"

Minutes later, they lay with their bodies pressed together in the spoon position, and Miyoko closed her eyes and allowed her strings to take over. Her strings would guide her consciousness in the realms still referred to as dreams.

***

When she opened her eyes, Winston no longer lay beside her. She rose and found him sitting cross-legged on the ground outside the ship, the creature three feet in front of him. Mist had turned to a fine drizzle and they were both shiny with rain. Neither seemed to notice. Yet when Miyoko appeared, Winston turned his head to look at her and the flat, round spots on the creature slid over its surface to point in her direction.

Winston gestured and said, "Miyoko, come look." He pointed at the ground in front of the creature. "We've communicated."

Between Winston and the creature, in the wet sand that never seemed to cling, she saw the words, "I learn you teach".

"How… you mean *it* wrote that? she asked.

"Yes. And it wants to be allowed to touch me."

"Winston! You mustn't – under no circumstances should you come into direct contact."

As though he hadn't heard her, Winston said, "The creature calls itself 'K'." His palm smoothed the sand, erasing the words, and using his index finger, he wrote 'You touch I hurt.'

A pseudopod extended, erased Winston's words, and replaced them with 'I did not want to hurt'. Then it erased again and wrote 'I not hurt you'. The pseudopod retracted and the creature became still, waiting in the drizzle.

Winston tilted his head back to speak directly to Miyoko, squinting his eyes against the falling moisture. "I have to allow it. This kind of situation is what we've been trained for. And I believe it can be trusted."

He leaned forward again and carved one word in the unearthly soil, "Yes".

The creature closed the short distance to Winston with a surprising rapidity. A new, more slender pseudopod reached out to touch the right side of Winston's head with supreme gentleness. Somewhere in Winston's mind he thought he heard, "You symmetrical…" Then another pseudopod protruded from the creature, making contact with the other side of Winston's head, millimeters above his left ear, and he distinctly heard, "... so two contacts are required. Do they cause you discomfort?"

"No. None at all. And I hear you quite clearly. Can you hear me?"

"Yes."

Miyoko witnessed the contact of an alien mind with her partner's with only a trace of anxiety. Within moments the two pseudopods retracted and Winston's eyes acquired a slight glaze as the creature undulated over to the ship, touching the surface with its main pseudopod. Winston remained in his sitting position, silent. With renewed concern, Miyoko said, "Winston!" but he reassured her, saying, "That was… incredible. How long were we in contact?"

"About ten seconds, I think. What happened?"

"I would have guessed more like ten minutes… K told me a great deal about itself. It possesses a surprisingly good understanding of our language and symbolism. Apparently K is sexless, reproducing by splitting off part of its body, like cell division but with something analogous to horizontal gene transfer, and on a much larger scale than any other creature I know of. However, K is familiar with sexual reproduction since virtually every life form on this planet uses it. But the crucial fact is K's species is unique. In fact *nothing* else on this planet reproduces in a way even remotely like it."

"That's unexpected. In any closed ecological system a spectrum of diversity generally evolves. Why would K's species be the only one to reproduce in that manner – almost as if it originated in some other ecosystem? I find that concerning."

"So did I. So I asked. K doesn't have a clear answer either. It speculates that perhaps its species was originally from another planet. These organisms don't keep records of any kind because their entire memories are passed from one generation to another when they reproduce. The trouble is, their origin on this planet was so long ago their memory may have changed, sort of like mutating genes. K's mental capacity is staggering, by the way."

"I suppose it must be the dominant organism on this planet. Is that true, do you think?"

"I think that's a good assumption. Would you like to ask K yourself?" Winston started to get up but Miyoko stopped him and paused a moment before replying.

"No. I haven't quite gotten over the chunk it took out of my leg. I'm not ready to give it another opportunity yet. By the way, what do you think it might have learned from you?"

Winston turned an impassive face toward the creature as it extended a tentative pseudopod over the threshold of the open hatch. "I don't know. It didn't ask many questions. But it did seem curious about the ship… It wanted to know how we got here, and asked me specifically about the Witten Device. I got the impression it was just asking to be polite."

***

They lay in the common berth, Winston on his back. The ship's hatch was closed. Miyoko wanted it that way. She pushed her fingertips through his brown hair, searching in vain for some sign of the alien's contact. "You really didn't feel anything?" she whispered.

"I felt the touch of K's pseudopods, of course, but nothing unusual. It was the actual communication that was so extraordinary – like conversing with someone in your mind – not external." He lowered his voice, traced the arch of her eyebrow, and added, "It was very intimate. I found myself wishing you could be part of it too."

***

The second communication session began as the first, but with Miyoko sitting next to Winston on the ground outside the ship. The drizzle had stopped, leaving a fog of supersaturated air, sauna warm. The physical contact between K and Winston was reestablished, and Winston began, "K, Miyoko would like to join us. Would that be possible?"

"Yes. I would like that." Two more thin pseudopods linked Miyoko to K, one on each temple. "Welcome, Miyoko. With your permission I will allow you to hear everything between Winston and myself and he will hear your thoughts as well. Is that acceptable?"

"Of course – thank you for asking. I think I will just listen for a while."

Winston began. "In our first session, you told me a little about yourself and your species. What would you like to know about us?"

"I learn from simple contact. It is enough."

"How do you mean? I ask questions and you answer. Don't you have any questions?"

"Yes – many – but asking them isn't necessary."

"I still don't know what you mean by that. Can you explain more fully?"

"Perhaps I must tell you more about my kind. We are hunters. As you know, there are numerous other species on this planet, none of which have intelligence beyond what is needed to survive. But each species possesses different requirements for survival, and consequently, different skills and behaviors. My species is adept at understanding those requirements, skills, and behaviors. That's what makes us such effective hunters. However, we only harvest and consume what is needed to sustain us." K paused. "You wonder why we are such skilled hunters. And that leads to the point about how we learn." Another pause. "The flesh of every species has its own taste. The taste is determined by its genetic codes. Genetic codes also contain information about an individual organism, and each cell contains varying amounts of information, but the most complete knowledge about the individual resides in the conglomeration of cells used to reason, to think. When we consume a prey, we decode, aggregate, and integrate every bit of that information. When we consume a prey, we learn where it spent the last three hours, the last three days, the last three years. We learn everything there is to know about its mate, where its mate might be found. We learn everything. In that way, we gain such a complete understanding of our prey that hunting more of them is effortless."

Winston struggled to understand and believe the full import of what he'd been told. He asked, "And what about what you did to Miyoko?"

"The sample of cells I took from her contained barely enough information to learn how to communicate with you, but that sample was enough to tell me you are highly advanced beings, far beyond what we normally consider prey."

"How many of you are there?"

K paused again, longer than before. "Our numbers are in balance with the number of our prey. They will be here soon."

The four slender pseudopods touching Winston and Miyoko became more slender, penetrating toward the tissue of their brains. They felt no pain – nothing that might activate a Guardian. Cells comprising muscle tissue were consumed first, the unsupported neurons and synapses of the peripheral and central nervous systems left intact; pale, lace-like gossamers. Guardians fell away, useless. Only then did K begin the consumption of neurons. In Winston's last sentient moments, he saw the clearing before the ship fill with undulating, formless creatures. And as the totality of his neurons diminished, so carefully and methodically consumed, so did his ability to cogitate, until consciousness flickered out.

***

K was satisfied. Two jumbled piles of etched bone, mixed with some organic-shaped metallic plastic objects, objects now identified as string implants, lay on the ground. The other members of the tribe, having each been given a small portion of the prey's flesh, explored the ship.

But most importantly, K understood the Witten Device, how it worked – and from where it came.

***

Winston's memories were assembled in chronological order, rebuilding the totality of his existence. As his final thoughts took their place like the utmost components topping a house of cards, consciousness reasserted itself.

He stood on the surface of the planet, a fine drizzle, almost mist, filling the air. Miyoko, motionless next to him, moved her hand into his. What he knew to be the voice of K echoed in his mind, saying, "You and Miyoko are in me now. All you once were, with the exception of your physical manifestation, I've reconstructed in my being from the information contained in your flesh."

A memory of what it felt like to experience panic tried to rise up in Winston's thoughts, but he suppressed it. To his astonishment, Miyoko asked, "If I exist only in you, and am merely a construct of my past, how could I ever experience anything new?"

"Through me. I will add my sensory input of some of the things I see, taste, smell, hear, even touch. And, to Winston, you are more than just a memory. In my consciousness, I allow the two of you to interact. But I control the degree of interaction. All creatures I've consumed, all who my forebears consumed down the ages, exist in me. Through me and all my descendents, you are now virtually immortal."

Winston said, "You say you will let us experience some of what you sense. Only some things?"

"Yes. It will be selective. You would not be able to

correlate everything I am capable of sensing. But I will integrate things into your awareness as though they are your own. Behold."

Winston's reality transformed. With an undulating, melting fluidity, the planet morphed into the interior of the ship. It had been changed. In Winston's memory, the interior had been barely large enough for himself and Miyoko – their sleeping quarters, galley, and instrumentation surrounding the central pillar housing the Witten Device. Now the interior was much larger. A new chamber curved off from the original circular room, much like the interior of a pseudopod, and Winston could see rows upon rows of what appeared to be large, bowl-shaped containers made of polished stone, each occupied by a creature exactly like K.

And K said, "This is what I see at this moment. We have modified your ship, and final preparations are being made."

Winston dreaded the answer to his next question. "Preparations for what?"

"For traveling to your planet of origin. Our numbers will increase there."

## About the Author

John N. Crain can most often be found within a thirty mile radius of Santa Fe, New Mexico.

Though he has had professional careers in the fine arts, astronomy, and computer science, in the moments between those fragments of time he considers real, he tends to write science fiction. He is currently working on numerous short stories, and two novels having to do with alternate universes.

His under-construction web site is:
www.treesonthemoon.com

# ENID
# AND THE OWLS

KT WAGNER

One foot, then the other. Enid Bailey shifts her weight back and forth. Standing too long locks up her knees, and it's become worse since the accident. From the bottom step of the shadowed porch, she peers into the dark. What kind of people don't leave a light on at night?

The moon is waning, but still bright. A night bird flaps past, briefly silhouetted. She recognizes the owl and smiles.

Up the stairs she trudges, lifts the iron ring and taps it against the door. The sound echoes on the other side of the door. The scent of lilacs clogs her nose and she stifles a sneeze. The faint licorice scent confirms it; the white lilacs are, Lemoine, the variety Miss Wilson requested.

Miss Wilson whispered to Enid about her wish to savour the perfume of Lemoine one last time. Each night, for a week now, right before her midnight cleaning shift at the seniors' home, Elysium Manor, Enid searched the neighbourhood for this exact variety.

Enid frowns. The blossoms are fading; she cannot wait another day to ask permission. Surely the homeowners will understand. Miss Wilson, the poor soul, shouldn't have to suffer another year.

She slips a pair of garden shears from her uniform pocket.

Bouquet cut, Enid unties her thin cotton apron, borrowed from the manor kitchen, and lays it on the ground. The faded stain on the front of her uniform is now exposed. She hesitates, swallows and reminds herself that no-one will notice on the dark streets.

Her fingers brush across the embroidered logo on the right breast pocket of her shirt—Tri-city Janitorial Services. Twenty-six years and an impeccable employee record at the Central City Residence. She'd taken pride in the job when others considered it a stop gap, or a stepping stone to something better. Not Enid, she loved her job. Maybe she should have explained that better? At the end, when she'd slowed down a little, they'd tossed her aside like she was worth nothing.

*Stop thinking about it*, she chides herself and tries to return her attention to the task at hand. She wraps the lilac bouquet in the apron and carefully straightens. Her bones pop and creak.

Despite arthritic joints she didn't log a single sick day in over twenty years, but did that count for anything? No, of course not. They were so kind on the surface, but within the soft words they were hard-hearted. She had to leave.

They offered her two choices: the night shift at Elysium Manor or they'd move her to her daughter's, all the way across the country to a place she'd never even visited. She picked the manor of course. She could still be of service.

They didn't even issue her a new uniform.

She first heard the owls at the Central City Residence, not long before her fall. It shames her to remember that owls called and she didn't answer, so she tells no one.

A lump rises in her throat. It's so unfair, but she's trying to get past it and make a difference where she is.

Sulphur-yellow street lights cast long shadows. She hobbles along the sidewalk, her cane tapping against crumbling cement. She is only a bit wobbly and doesn't use it at work. They might misunderstand and the vacuum keeps her steady enough.

A man walking his dog nods and pauses. She smiles, nods back and continues on her way.

***

Rounding the corner, Enid glares at the crooked sign for Elysium Manor--such a pretentious name. The nursing home is a one-story building with a flat roof, tiny windows and dented aluminum siding. A twenty-foot laurel hedge shields the neighbours from the eyesore.

Slipping in the staff entrance, Enid pauses in the dark kitchen, and arranges the flowers in an industrial-size metal measuring cup to deliver later.

Her job here is not particularly hard, vacuuming and light dusting mostly. At first, she was concerned about the noise of the vacuum, but most of the residents are either deep sleepers or turn off their hearing aids at night. Only a handful are awake during her shift, her night owls. She smiles. They assure her the noise from the vacuum isn't a problem. Only Abagail, the night nurse, seems bothered, but she's always grumpy. Enid finds it best to avoid her.

The work soothes. She's only responsible for the corridors and common areas. In the heart of the night they are deserted and dark. Sometimes, despite the ache in her bones, she fancies herself young again. Those dreams help pass the time.

On her break, she delivers the lilacs to Miss Wilson. The former gardener resembles a snowy owl with her puff of white hair and pale, desiccated skin.

Enid places the bouquet on a metal trolley and pushes it up to the bedrail. Miss Wilson struggles onto her elbows and leans toward the blossoms. Enid longs to help her, but it's strictly against the rules for cleaning staff to touch patients. She's proud of being a model employee.

She squints around the room. Boxes are piled in the corner behind the late Mrs. Rosenberg's bed. The pile obscures half the window. A surge of anger tightens Enid's chest. It's inhumane the way some residents are treated. This may be one of the city's charity homes, but that doesn't excuse the callousness on display.

She misses Mrs. Rosenberg, her burrowing owl. The poor woman pined for the books she loved. On breaks Enid read to Mrs. Rosenberg from novels she found in the tiny resident library. It happened in the middle of a chapter from Jane Eyre. The old woman sighed a contented sigh and a radiance lit her face, and she was gone. Enid smiles at the memory of Mrs. Rosenberg.

Miss Wilson smiles back and exhales a rattling sigh. She falls back onto her pillow, cradling a blossom against her chest. Her face glows. "Thank-you my dear. Thank-you."

It's hard to respond. Miss Wilson's eyes flutter close. Enid's eyes are moist. "You're welcome," she whispers.

Miss Wilson appears almost transparent. Enid watches for a minute, then carefully backs out of the room and closes the door.

***

Enid always feels displaced and confused after tending to one of her owls. Pushing the vacuum around the front hall calms the crashing waves in her head. Her uniform is wrinkled and her apron damp. She smooths the material with her free hand and steers the vacuum back into the corridor between the resident rooms. Her shoulders hunch and her head bows as she shuffles along.

At times like this the injury bothers her the most. The doctors told her she'd have to learn to live with the pain. It's a miracle you survived a fall down a flight of stairs, they said, like she should be thankful to be alive and not complain.

Mrs. Peterson's keening cry is haunting and sad, like a great gray owl, and it tugs Enid away from her own misery. A flash of anger straightens Enid's back. Nurse Abigail's ability to ignore the crying, night after night, speaks to the woman's missing soul.

It would be heartless to wait until after her shift to visit Mrs. Peterson.

"Have you found her?" Mrs. Peterson asks when Enid enters her room.

"I'm sorry, I still need to call the number the lady on Bracken Avenue mentioned," she whispers, though she wonders why she bothers; Mrs. Peterson's roommate sleeps like the dead.

The roommate arrived two days ago and Enid still hasn't learned her name. There are many residents she doesn't know because they keep daylight hours. A chill finger of regret runs down her spine and her fists clench.

She misses the dayshift and the sunshine.

"Please, please call tonight." Mrs. Peterson's reedy voice echoes through the room.

Enid longs to wrap her arms around the old woman and comfort her. "I'll try."

She met Mrs. Peterson her first night at Elysium Manor. Some of the others liked to chitchat, but the frail woman got straight to the point. "Find my daughter. I was never a good mother, but I want her to know that I always loved her. It's my only wish."

The address she provided was a few blocks further than Enid normally ventured. When she finally found it late one evening, the woman who answered the door laughed. "Mrs. Peterson? Pretty sure that old bitty died a decade ago. Her daughter moved to Long Point. Check the phone book."

Enid hesitates to telephone in the middle of the night, and Nurse Abagail is sure to find out about an unauthorized long-distance call.

Mrs. Peterson's mouth stretches wide and an undulating cry fills the room.

Enid abandons her vacuum in the room and heads down the hall to the office. Surely, Nurse Abagail will understand.

With trembling fingers, she punches in the number from memory.

"Hello?" The woman at the other end of the line sounds tired and annoyed. "Who is this? I have call display. Why is Elysium Manor calling me in the middle of the night?"

Enid repeats Mrs. Peterson's message quickly and waits. There is a sound like a sob, then silence. The silence expands.

Finally, a chilly response. "You must have your Petersons mixed up. My mother is long in the ground."

A click and the line disconnects.

Enid sighs. Another dead end.

She hurries through the silent hall to tell Mrs. Peterson they have to keep looking.

Nurse Abagail waits outside the old lady's door. "Enid, why don't you lie down for a bit?" She doesn't sound grumpy; she sounds tired.

Enid stops in confusion.

Nurse Abagail holds open the door.

Mrs. Peterson isn't in her bed.

"What have you done with Mrs. Peterson?" Enid clutches the door frame.

Nurse Abagail shakes her head. "You've outdone yourself tonight. I found the lilacs after a nice young man called in with a concern about a resident wandering the streets. And, why hide flowers in an empty room?"

Enid blinks. She stares at her vacuum. For the briefest moment, it looks like a walker. She blinks again.

"The lilacs were for Miss Wilson. I'll apologize to the homeowners."

"We don't have a Miss—"

Nurse Abagail is always grumbling about something.

A new voice fills the corridor. Enid tilts her head. It sounds like a screech owl.

## About the Author

KT Wagner loves reading and writing speculative fiction. Occasionally she ventures out of her writers' cave to spend an hour or two blinking against the daylight, or reacquainting herself with family and friends. Several of her short stories are published and she is working on a sci-fi horror novel. She puts pen to paper in Maple Ridge, B.C.

KT can be found on Twitter @KT_Wagner and online at www.northernlightsgothic.com.

# THE YELLOW DOOR

ISHA RO

The neighbors were taken aback by its sudden appearance. One day, there was a proper, glossy black door on house number three, a house as posh as all the others. The next day the "For Sale" sign was removed and the street had woken up to the yellow monstrosity.

They made disapproving clucking noises when they caught sight of it. *How ghastly,* they thought, their upper lips curled over. *As if we live in any old sort of bohemian ghetto.* They were eager to see who had moved in so they could show their displeasure in person. But there was something about that door that seemed… off. It made their skin crawl and their stomachs heave.

Pippa Montrose, however, would not be swayed by a little nausea. Perpetually bored and very nosy, she walked boldly up the steps, her signature bread and butter pudding in tow, to rap on the door and discover what kind of person she would now be forced to exchange pleasantries with of a morning or afternoon. She was sure it would be the wrong sort, some kind of new money, maybe even Arabs, lord knows they're so gaudy. Best to get in front of it and let them know that this wasn't the kind of neighborhood to condone this sort of rubbish.

If anyone had been watching, they would have seen Pippa trip gaily up the steps and knock confidently on the door. They would have seen the door slide open just a crack and watch Pippa stiffen like a board, abruptly dropping her baked goods on the floor. If they could have seen her face, they would have seen the horror etched on it, her mouth locked in rictus, her hair whitening slowly from root to ends. They would have seen her step oddly, as if fighting her own body, through the slender opening. That's what they would have seen if they'd been watching.

When Pippa's husband, Charles, came home to an empty house and the telltale signs of baking in the kitchen, he rolled his eyes and chuckled at his wife's ability to meddle in other people's business. But by 8pm when she should have had dinner on the table, he began to be concerned. By 11pm, he stormed up the steps to the yellow door to find out what on earth she could still be doing at the new neighbor's. He, too, knocked confidently on the solid wood. He, too, went rigid as he faced the slimmest of openings. His skin went gray and sagged from beneath his eyes as they widened, his feet sliding him forwards, over the threshold. And, like his wife, he never came back out.

After that, odd lights would come on at night behind the opaque windows of the yellow-doored house, deeply red and…throbbing. There were also sounds. A keening like a mother who had lost her child; the deep-throated growls of a man in the throes of a murderous rage; a thump-thump-thumping like a heart hidden under the floorboards, refusing to die. The neighbors heard these things as clearly as if they were happening in their own rooms. They tossed and turned in their beds, waking up drenched with sweat, the remnants of forgotten nightmares clinging to their skin.

Then, other strange things began to happen.

Henry Tennant glanced at the yellow door on his way to his law firm's glass-walled offices and his heart began to race. He started to sweat. His breath became shallow. Only the ringing of his cellphone jolted him out of his strange reverie, his meetings missed, his hours unbilled. Disoriented, he glanced towards the sky to see the sun sinking slowly to its slumber, although it hadn't yet risen when he had left home. He shook his head, trying to free himself of the fog behind his eyes, his muscles aching strangely as he walked away, dazed and confused.

When Mary Wentworth strolled past the yellow door on her way to tea at Harrod's, she looked at it sideways, trying to surreptitiously catch a movement from within the house – a twitching of curtains, a shadow across a window. A glimpse of who might be inside. She was roused back to the present by the cold fingers of rain falling on her shoulders, her hair drenched, her makeup running, the street swathed in the velvet embrace of darkest night. Her forehead would have wrinkled in confusion if it was still able to move. Instead, she blinked what felt like sleep out of her eyes and stumbled home, all plans for shopping and tea and gossip forgotten.

Jane Granger walked past the yellow door, her arms laden with last season's fashions for charity shops and she looked straight at it. And she remembered.

She remembered walking through the yellow door and being greeted by a man with eyes deep like black pools of smoke and a yellowed grin full of sharpened teeth. She remembered his smell, the overpowering scent of lilies left to rot and how he'd led her inside, blood bubbling up from where he'd kissed her. She remembered how his hand felt like soft, dying tree bark but, at the same time, like a vice in which her bones were caught.

She remembered seeing Pippa and Charles with goat-like horns that had ripped through their foreheads, their bodies transformed by crossing the threshold. Blood had dried in trails down their faces like tears. The backs of their arms heavy with hair, their feet cloven hooves, writhing in anguish on the forest floor, reaching for her.

Jane and Henry and Mary and the others, they all remembered removing every stitch of clothing and doing strange and terrible things in a dense and darkened wood. Clawing and biting and killing like animals, tearing skin from bones, dancing in blood. Sexual congress with wild half-beasts and grinning demons. Feeling pain, inflicting pain, sharp and quick and dull and throbbing. Howling like wolves at the moon, rutting with anything that moved, eating and being eaten, blood smeared across their teeth.

And, most horrifying of all, they remembered that they'd enjoyed it.

Later they would discover scratches and bruises in the most unusual places, parts of their bodies tender to the touch, scars where before there had been none. And they were afraid. Of what they had done, of what had been done to them.

Of wanting more.

Slowly, one by one, they began to seek out the door, wanting to see it and not wanting to. They stood in the street in clusters and crowds, afraid to pass through it but desperate to be near it, swaying gently against each other in a shared stupor, their eyes blank and unseeing. Dinners were left bubbling over on the stove, children forgotten at school, bills left unpaid, jobs ignored. Eventually, one thing or other would propel them back to reality and they would shuffle resignedly home, each unaware of the others around them.

Exhausted and terrorized, vivid dreams of blackness and horror plaguing every moment, they eventually turned on each other.

Jane drove a steak knife suddenly through her husband's eye as they sat at the dinner table, staring listlessly at empty plates. She drank a bottle of drano as a digestif.

Henry studied his sleeping wife for a while before smothering her beneath his pillow and then shooting himself in the head with his gun. The shot rang out sharp in the still of the night but no one batted an eyelash at its report.

John Turlinton, from two doors down, beat his girlfriend savagely with a Le Creuset frying pan, but not before she'd boiled a pot of water and thrust it at his back. He crawled to his front door, his skin bubbling and crackling like a pig's on a spit, only to find Mary there, her chef's knife in hand. She plunged it through his lungs before slitting her own throat.

One by one, house by house, the neighbours ripped themselves and each other to shreds.

In the morning, as their broken and bloodied bodies lay where they'd fallen, the sun rose on the small, exclusive enclave that stank of death.

A 'For Sale' sign stood on the lawn of house number

three. A house as posh as all the others, with a proper, understated, glossy black door.

## About the Author

Isha Ro is a Jamaican writer living in Berlin. Her apartment is stuffed to the brim with a large Czech, an oversized stuffed monkey and an imaginary Golden Retriever called George. She writes creepy stories and funny stories and both of these involve an inordinate amount of murder.

You can read more of her work at
www.theprosateur.com.

# NO LAUGHING MATTER

PHIL TEMPLES

I'm kicking back in my office chair about to make a serious dent in a vanilla donut frosted with sprinkles, when Gladys slaps a note in front of me. Without so much as a "hello" she starts to walk back to her desk. I don't know what I did to tick her off. Gladys has been giving me the cold shoulder all week. Perhaps it's because I forgot to buy her flowers for Secretary's Day. Nowadays they call it National Administrator's Day or some such politically correct bullshit.

I put down the donut and examine the note, but I can't make hide nor hair of Gladys' hen scratches. I suspect she's doing it to antagonize me.

"Uh, Gladys?"

"Yes?"

I hold up her note, and shrug my shoulders as if to say, 'W.T.F.?'

"Another one over in Forest Mills, Phil." She spells it out for me. "Classic white face. Bus stop. Perp tried to get a cheap laugh by taking a fall. When that didn't work he jerked off in front of a little girl. A passer-by heard the vic screaming and chased the perp into Bryant Park. Sheriff's deputy took the statement. That's his number."

The phone number is the only thing I can make out.

*Dep. Samuel… no, Stephen Levine… Hell! I guess it doesn't matter. At least I got the number.*

"Classic white face, huh? That makes three this week in Forest Mills." The response comes from my partner, Detective Antony Perazzi. In addition to our regular duties, Ton and I are currently assigned to a special anti-terrorism joint task force.

I reach over, pick up my notebook, and begin to recite details from a case last week. "Yeah. Last one was Thursday. Same M.O.: falling down, then exposing himself to kids at a school bus stop. But that perp was an Auguste with a red wig."

"An Aug, huh?"

I call up Google Maps and look at the area in question.

That's when it hits me. "Ton, you suppose there's an 'alley' of 'em holed up in the park?"

"What makes you think that?"

I hold up my badge and display it to Tony. "Well, jerkoff, you don't get to be a Lieutenant Detective by bein' a slouch!"

Ton throws a paper wad at me, but it misses by a mile.

"After our teleconference, let's go check out the park."

***

Tony and I settle in the oversized, plush conference room chairs to participate in the briefing by the Department of Homeland Security. In the wake of numerous high-profile clown attacks, clowns are now considered domestic terrorists. They're outlawed in about a dozen states. (Not in ours, unfortunately.) Homeland Security tracks them like any Al Qaeda inspired terrorist. DHS is leaving no stone unturned; even the run-of-the-mill clowns—the ones that expose themselves, loiter or commit petty crimes—are now tracked on a watch list. It's likely that our perp in Forest Mills is on the list. If not, he'll soon be. The last generation of clowns—the conventional circus clowns or the Shriners clowns—have hung up their rubber noses and wigs and found other vocations. But I'd be surprised if a few of those haven't gone rogue.

The moderator introduces himself as Special Agent Francis McCordy from the FBI's Philadelphia office. He could be a male model from some fashion magazine. He's that good-looking. There's a female agent, too. Alice Walker, from the Bureau of Alcohol, Tobacco, Firearms, Explosives, and Clowns. She's a real looker, too. I bet neither one of them has ever walked the beat.

"...There have been dozens of credible threats made against schools in Philadelphia, St. Louis, and Atlanta in the past week. They're all associated with the recent wave of people dressing and posing on social media as clowns to frighten and harass."

"Are there any common traits?" The question comes from a New York City cop.

"There are some similarities in the targets," replies the G-man. "Most of them talk about blowing up schools, or axing teachers and students in lavatories. Their appearances vary. Some of the costumes are more Halloweenish in appearance—that is, the psycho-killer and evil clown archetypes. We think they're related."

Walker posts a photo of one of the perps in a separate screen. He's done up in a classic psycho-killer mask, something made popular by a television series, *American Horror Story: Freak Show.*

*That clown is one scary sombitch for sure.*

G-man rambles on. He mentions the latest social media images are available via the NCIC Clown Database. Tony scribbles down the URL in his notepad.

"Local police departments are actively investigating the threats and trying to find out who is responsible for them, while school districts are working with police to ensure students' safety when schools reopen after Labor Day. If there are no more questions..."

***

After a brief stop at a Starbucks, we head out to Bryant Park in the suburb of Forest Mills. It's about a 40-minute drive. On the way, I call Deputy *Stan Levitz* (Thanks to Gladys' poor handwriting, my guess wasn't even close!) and get more particulars of the case. He agrees to meet us at the park.

Levitz also suspects an alley of clowns in the vicinity. He's received a second report of a sad face accompanied by a psycho face lurking in the community. Says the psycho disappeared, but the sad sack hung around and performed a juggling act with some bowling ball pins. When he started urinating against a tree, the parents in the neighborhood decided enough was enough. They chased his ass for a couple of blocks until sad sack-o-shit high-tailed it into the woods near the park.

We pull into the parking lot at the park. An unmarked cruiser is sitting in the far end. Its blue lights are faintly visible behind the grill. Ton and I pull up alongside.

"You Deputy Stanley Levitz?"

We make introductions. Stan asks if we want to briefly reconnoiter the area. I say, sure. I figure we might get lucky and find some clown droppings. Clowns are a sloppy lot. They frequently litter, sometimes leaving the tools of their trade lying around haphazardly.

After a bit, I ask Stan: "You see action in the Gulf?" He seems ex-military to me.

"Fallujah," he replies.

"Wow, that was some heavy shit. Ton was stateside. Fort Hood. I spent eight months in Desert Storm myself. Kuwait. Nothing compared to your tour, that's for sure."

"Yeah. I don't like to talk about it very much."

The three of us walk in silence.

The park contains a hundred acres of heavily wooded land. I figure their camp (if, in fact, there is one) is set up along the outskirts, perhaps near a source of water. I check Google Maps again. There's a small stream not far from our current location. I suggest that we head toward it.

About a half-mile in, we come across a lightly worn path. We follow it. Along the way, I spot a clue: a bright, red bulb lying on the ground.

"Hey," I whisper. "Got a nose here."

We fall into recon formation. Stan has the combat experience and he instinctively takes lead. Tony is in the rear, scanning for hostiles. I reach inside my jacket to feel for the reassuring presence of my Sig Saur pistol. We're all a little on edge.

Suddenly we come up to a clearing.

*There!* An alley of clowns. I count at least two dozen of them. All kinds: white faces, Augustes, sad faces, tramps and hobos. I count a dozen tents, and two mobile home trailers. There are five mimes off to one side. It's odd to see them here. Most clowns can't stand mimes. I guess hard times make for interesting bedfellows.

A few seconds one of the perps—an Auguste—spots us and starts honking on a toy horn. The other clowns hear his alarm and see us. They begin to scatter. Before I can give chase, I feel a warm trickle of liquid splashing on to my back and shoulders.

*What the--?!*

One of the sad faces is about twenty feet above me in a tree. He's pissing down on me. *Disgusting*! I wish I had brought along my taser. If I had, I'd stick that sucker in his piss stream, turn it on, and watch him shriek in agony at receiving 50,000 volts right in the ole' pecker…

Ton's warning interrupts my thoughts.

"LOOK OUT, PHIL!"

I turn around just in time to see a bowling ball coming at me. I quickly duck to one side. It misses me. Stan runs over to the clown who heaved it. The perp holds his ground. Stan grabs for him, but he jerks to and fro, avoiding Stan's clutch. It's almost comical to watch. After a few seconds, Stan stops moving. Then the perp stops moving, too. That's when Stan cold-cocks him.

*Score one for the good guys.*

Off to my right, Ton has his hands full with a female white face perp. She's squeezing a bulb in her hand and squirting some sort of liquid at Ton out of a large sunflower pinned to her lapel. Ton frowns as the spray hits him squarely in the face. I'm guessing it's not water. Just then, a small perp on a tricycle comes up behind Ton and rams into his leg. *Ouch*!

While this is going on, I start to give chase after a mime that's standing nearby. Then I catch movement out of the corner of my eye.

*It's got to be their leader!*

The face is grotesque. He's the scariest-looking son of a

bitch I've ever laid eyes on. He's a goddamn thing of nightmares. If that mug doesn't give you a full-blown case of coulrophobia, nothing will.

The perp's face is painted with distorted eyes that drip blood. He sports oversized teeth. The wig is matted. Large chunks of hair appear to be missing. The outfit itself is in tatters, and stained in vomit.

Suddenly, it dawns on me: I've seen this guy before. I'm staring at the same mug from the briefing!

The next few seconds seem to go by in slow motion. I see psycho clown bring his arm around from behind his back. He's holding some kind of knife. I reach for my gun, but the perp is faster. With a quick, jerking motion he unleashes the projectile in my direction. That's when the lights go out.

***

"He's awake."

I open my eyes. My vision is blurry and my left arm feels numb. My head hurts, too. I'm in a hospital bed. I see the face of my partner, Ton, looming above me.

"Obviously, I'm not dead cuz I wouldn't be starin' up at your ugly puss if I was."

I also see Captain of Detectives Patrick "Patty" Murphy along with Chief James Stockton waiting off to the side.

"It's a good thing you got a thick skull," says Ton. "That psycho did a number on ya, pal. Drilled ya right in the side of the head with some kinda Ninja star. Penetrated part of your brain, they said. Let's hope it's the part you don't use."

"Lieutenant, it's good to have you back," says Patty. "The doctors said it was 'touch and go' for a few hours but they think you'll make a full recovery."

"Thanks, Cap'n," I reply. "Wh—what happened to the perp that nailed me?"

"You can thank your new friend, Deputy Stan Levitz," said the Chief. "Levitz saved your life. The guy sure knows his combat medicine." Stockton adds, "That nasty goon face won't be terrorizing anymore. Levitz put three slugs dead center in the perp's heart. Good kill. In fact, he's being nominated for the Medal of Valor."

"Not only that," interrupted Ton, "When you've recuperated, ATFEC wants to give you a special commendation for sniffing out that alley. That group was the nexus of an interstate operation. They tapped into a nearby electric pole and fiber, and were enjoying all the comforts of home, so to speak: TV, Wi-Fi, and high-speed internet service. A lot of harassing emails and videos were coming from that camp. You hit the mother lode."

I can't believe I'm hearing them correctly. *Commendation*? "Really? Okay, stop clowning around, you guys."

**About the Author**

Phil Temples lives in Watertown, Massachusetts, and works as a computer systems administrator at a university. He's had over a 130 short fiction stories published in print and online journals. His full-length murder-mystery novel, 'The Winship Affair' is available from Blue Mustang Press as well as two new books: a short story anthology, 'Machine Feelings' and paranormal horror mystery, 'Helltown Chronicles,' from Big Table Publishing.

# MY BETTER HALF

MARK BLICKLEY

People who see me must think I'm eccentric, emotionally disturbed, or lonely. People who speak with me have told me that I'm an obnoxious, good for nothing bastard, a nasty prick, but I don't give a fuck what anyone thinks. I don't even care who reads this damned notebook. My name, Andrew Tremper, is right on the cover for all to see.

It all started about nine years ago. I was shacking up with this girl who was what they call a "modern dancer." We lasted a little under a year together. Her name was Miriam and she went to some artsy fartsy college up in New England to study THE DANCE. When she returned to New York she joined a dance company called Dervishing Divas. I met her at a performance on Manhattan's Upper West Side.

I was confused. I'm an educated man and I know what a dervish is—it's spinning around, out of control. But the Divas didn't spin. Hell, they barely moved. For over an hour all they did was lift a leg or move an arm or twitch their head every few minutes while electronic music slammed into our ears and pulsing lights irritated our eyes. The Dervishing Divas sucked, but Miriam looked awfully good in her low cut leotard, and I could she that she had the rounded buttocks of a thoroughbred horse.

I don't even remember how I got to a Dervishing Diva performance or where I heard about them, except that back then I used to make the rounds of a lot of inexpensive arts events because there was always lots of women and I was posturing as an arts enthusiast, a good looking, well built arts enthusiast. Hell, I remember the night I nailed Miriam. I had to put up with hours of her artspeak about how the Divas don't dance, they manipulate movement and shit like that. Well, let me tell you, she moved like a worm with a match under it later that night and a lot of nights that followed.

When she finally skipped out on me, the bitch left me a going away present—a life size cardboard cut-out of myself. On a note pinned to its crotch she said she had it made because talking to the cutout was the only time she could have an adult conversation with me, expose her feelings without being ridiculed, cut-off or ignored. The note said a helluva lot more than that, it was a freakin' manifesto, but you get the idea. It was a real artsy exit, don't you think? And probably the highlight of her creative career. I mean, just imagine all the thinking, planning and execution involved in trying to make me feel like a complete shit.

I was going to throw the damned thing out, but I grew sort of attached to it. She did pick a pretty decent photo of me to enlarge in cardboard, although I've always thought of myself as somewhat taller than I am. Standing back to back with the cutout proves we're both the exact height, five feet ten and three quarters of an inch. That sonofabitch dancer nailed me down to three quarters of an inch. In her manifesto she predicted I'd keep the life size cutout because I was so in love with myself. Miriam was wrong. I kept it to show the other broads I bang the monument of obsessive love given to me by a former member of the Dervishing Divas. The girls I take up to my apartment all seem to be impressed, so I guess Miriam's cruelty backfired on her. How's that saying go about a last laugh?

I kept the cardboard cut-out of myself inside my apartment for about three or four years. It made its world debut at a stupid party thrown by a woman I was involved with who lived in Hoboken. The point of the party was that no one could speak. Everybody had to write these responses, keep them in their pockets, and then show them to other guests when communication was desired. We were kind of like idiotic mimes without makeup. I feel like an ass even admitting that I've attended parties that, but hey, in a time of AIDS, artsy babes are the most liberal and liberated, so I played the game to win the prize. Sue me. It's better than sitting home and choking the chicken in front of adult video rentals although that, too, has its moments.

I cut up a few garbage bags and wrapped them around my cardboard cut-out that I named Sir Andrew. As I pulled the plastic around Sir Andrew's head, it felt as if I was trying to suffocate myself, which is ridiculous because I don't hate me. I pulled the plastic off Sir Andrew and decided to take him outside in all his glory. I figured I'd allow other people to enjoy twice the pleasure of our handsome face.

I had to carry my cardboard cut-out of myself down to the PATH train station at Thirty-third Street. PATH trains are subways that link New York City with New Jersey; and man did I get some bizarre reactions to carrying a life size cut-out of myself under my arm as I crossed the state line beneath the Hudson River. I dug the attention.

The reason why I decided to take Sir Andrew—I'm just plain old Andrew—to the party was because I'll be damned if I'll spend my time writing out silly shit on slips of paper just to appease some piece of ass. If they want me to be silent at a party, fine, they can talk to my life-sized cardboard cut-out, Sir Andrew. He won't answer them back.

Sir Andrew was the hit of the party. A gorgeous redhead even slipped me her phone number when her hostess wasn't watching because she wanted to hook up with the "creative genius" that had turned the party's conceit into what she said was a new art form, or some crap like that, yet all I did at the party was smoke some pot, down glasses of great cognac that the label said was made by monks, and eat like a pig. Whenever anyone approached me with their little fuckin' witty remarks on paper I'd shrug, shake my head, and point to Sir Andrew, who I propped up in a corner of the living room. So there you have it, the secrets of a creative genius. My mother used to yell at me that if I kept my mouth shut people wouldn't know how stupid I was. I guess the old bag was right. Anyway, tragedy befell me and Sir Andrew later that evening. I had planned to spend the night with my girlfriend, but she caught me making out with the redhead in the bathroom and pitched a fit. That's when the silent party turned into screams. I told her to shut up and stop running the integrity of her party, to pull something out of her fuckin' pocket for me to read if there was something she wanted to say.

The redhead immediately ran off and shortly afterwards my girlfriend kicked me out of her apartment. I grabbed Sir Andrew and staggered my way back towards the PATH station. I was really loaded; that bitch should not have driven me out of her home. Before I even made it over to the subway, a Hoboken cop gave me a summons for pissing in the street. I think I even accidentally sprayed a bit on poor Sir Andrew.

I had a hard enough time navigating through the streets and train turnstiles, but with Sir Andrew tucked under my arm it became damn near impossible. My cardboard cut-out smashed into telephone poles, parked cars, fire hydrants, as well as other pedestrians, and was nearly decapitated by closing subway doors. By the time we arrived home, Sir Andrew was bent, ripped, crumpled and stained. He looked exactly the way I felt. He slipped out of my hands as I flopped onto my bed.

When I woke up the next afternoon the first thing I saw was Sir Andrew, face up on the floor, next to my bed. He looked scary. It was as if I was looking in a mirror at a decaying, diseased image of myself. My first impulse was to crush my cut-out and toss it into the garbage, but the idea of trashing myself like that was too disturbing. That was when I realized how attached I'd become to the fuckin' thing.

I couldn't keep the cut-out, but I wouldn't throw it out either, until I could replace it. That's when I remembered walking past this porno palace right off of Times Square that advertised they could make life-sized cut-outs from photos, although the sample displays were all these gross looking naked people with bloated breasts and shriveled shlongs. They reminded me of my first experience at a nudist beach. I was about fifteen years old and was expecting to see all these incredibly hot babes jiggling about, playing volleyball, stretched out in the sand flashing more than just a smile. What a disgusting shock to discover that the nudists were mostly guys, middle-aged or even older, and the women on the beach looked liked my Mom's friends, or like our neighbors.

Anyway, I set up a timer on my camera and took fresh portraits of myself in my favorite outfits and picked out the best one. The guy at the porno palace couldn't believe that my balls weren't at least hanging out through my zipper. He charged me eighty-seven dollars and change and did a beautiful job. When I picked it up I noticed something quite interesting. My cardboard facial expression had a really strange look to it. I've since heard it described as compassionate, concerned, thoughtful and affectionate. The truth was that my expression was affected by total anxiety. It was the first time I had ever used my camera timer, the first time I ever took pictures of myself and I didn't think I was going to pull it off. I was too embarrassed to ask someone to take multiple portraits of me because they might think I was some kind of conceited, narcissistic bastard.

I liked having the new, updated version of Sir Andrew with me. Because of Saint Andrew's success at the Hoboken party, I decided to regularly ferry it out in public. And let me tell you, it attracted and engaged more female strangers than if I had been walking the most adorable puppy in Manhattan. I did notice, however, that when talking with these curious and inquisitive women they seemed to be paying more attention to my cardboard face rather than to my real face that was sputtering out words of charm and profundity.

The first question I was always asked was, of course, why do I have a life-size cut-out of myself? My answer would vary according to the appearance of the inquisitor. If guys asked me I would usually say something like my girlfriend is going out of town and couldn't bear to be without me for even a day, so she forced me to clone myself so I could travel everywhere she went. Or I would feign shock that they hadn't heard about the terrorist attack in Florence and that they needed an immediate model to replace the recently exploded statue of David, so I was on my way to Federal Express Sir Andrew to the Italian authorities, you know, stuff like that.

When young women asked me the same question my response was dependent on how they looked. If I wasn't attracted to the questioner I'd give them the same answer I gave the guys. If the woman looked like she had potential, I'd say something romantic like I was on my way to launch this cardboard representation of myself into the Hudson River, not unlike a Viking funeral pyre, because my dreams of trying to connect with true love had died, or my response would be something humbly humorous, like I decided to invest all my negative traits into this cut-out and was on my way to burn it in a sacrificial fire of repentance and purification, or some shit like that. You get the idea.

Funny thing, it turned out women didn't invest any of my negative traits into Sir Andrew---they did the exact opposite. Sometimes I'd bang babes that I swear were more in love with my cardboard self than with me. I remember one girl insisting that I prop the cut-out by the bed and keep the lights on so that she could see Sir Andrew while we did the nasty. There certainly are a lot of freaks out there, but freaks are the most fun in bed.

Sir Andrew was pretty good for me in more ways than just the babe department. I never needed a scale. When I'd start to pork up a little all I had to do was compare myself with the cardboard stud and it would force me to keep myself in check. I had to maintain the same handsome and appealing appearance as Sir Andrew because my worst nightmare would be that one day I'd be cruising the streets with Sir Andrew and no one would recognize that it was a life sized cut-out of me. Call it vanity if you want, but I call it a fight against nostalgia. I don't ever want Sir Andrew to represent my glory days---he must be representative of the here and now. And it's more important to me now than ever because that schmuck of mayor, Guiliani, has cleaned up the Times Square area and replaced porno shops with all the cartoon crap and family entertainments. Even my cardboard cut-out maker, Leon Sasha, was driven out of his Peep Show Paradise months ago and I've been unable to track him down.

I take Sir Andrew with me almost everywhere I go these days. Aside from his talent for attracting women, I discovered that he also supplies me with peace and safety when I travel home to Manhattan after working in one of the sleaziest neighborhoods in Brooklyn. All the fruitcakes, psychos and homeless assholes seem to fall instantly in love with Sir Andrew. I just lean back in my subway seat, close my eyes, and hold up the cut-out like a shield while some lunatic mutters away at it instead of pulling out a knife or hassling me about money. They tell the cardboard all about their wildest and sickest thoughts, experiences, confessions and actually seem to find comfort from that stupid look on Sir Andrew's face.

But the truth is, I'm starting to get a little pissed over all the attention paid Sir Andrew. Why the fuck does everybody love him so much? Why is he more important to people than I am? I mean, if I don't take care of him, protect him, he could easily be destroyed because he's so goddamned fragile even a little moisture could melt his compassionate smile into a sneer and ruin him! Ruin us!

What started out as a gimmick to attract attention to myself has really boomeranged into a gimmick that diverts attention away from me. Sometimes I feel like I'm the prop and that my cardboard image carts me around to help me keep in touch with the rest of humanity. To be honest I guess I'd like to be more like Sir Andrew. I've noticed that I have a tendency to sprinkle profanities and slang into my speech in order to bolster my image as a strong man, but Sir Andrew is completely silent and no one, man or woman, has ever questioned his strength or manliness. And he really seems to be able to help people with their problems because he listens to them and stares them in the face when they're talking to him.

In some ways I sort of admire Sir Andrew, but it's kind of hard to change when your role model is yourself.

## About the Author

Mark Blickley is the author of *Sacred Misfits* (Red Hen Press). His text based art collaboration with artist Amy Bassin, D*ream Streams*, was featured as an art installation at the 5th Annual NYC Poetry Festival and published in *Columbia Journal of Literature and Art.* Their new collaboration was published as a text based art chapbook, *Weathered Reports, Trump Surrogate Quotes From the Underground* (Moria Books, Chicago). Blickley is a proud member of the Dramatists Guild and PEN American Center.

# DINNER PARTY

ASHLEY LIBEY

She stood as still as she could. Her hands trembled, and she couldn't quite catch her breath. She was lightheaded and nauseous. Her mother swung the axe for the last time and then stood quietly, looking down at the ground, unaware that her daughter was still behind her. The thing was there, laying still now. Not moving. No longer making those awful noises.

Abby shifted slightly. The taffeta of her dress crinkled, and her mother turned. A lock of hair had come loose from her mother's chignon and hung, curled by her cheek.

"Abby, you should have gone back inside when I told you to." Her mother sounded tired and matter of fact. She closed the distance between them and put an arm around Abby's shoulders, careful to hold the axe slightly away from her own bright pink cocktail dress. Abby's heart slowed just a bit. She leaned her face into her mother's warm stomach, the fabric of her mother's dress somehow still immaculate. The fence was splattered with the same reeking, black tar that clung to the blade of the axe.

Abby peeked past her mother at the thing on the ground. It still lay perfectly still. Abby's heart raced, and she felt nauseous all over again seeing the body once more. It's back looked as though it had been broken. She was sure it would have never bent that way while alive. It was covered in scales the exact color of the dead fish her brother had made her look at by the river last week.

"It's dead now," her mother said. She saw where Abby was looking. She turned Abby away and began to walk carefully toward the house, ensuring her stilettos wouldn't sink too far into the muddy ground. Abby glanced back. Her mother's warm hand cupped Abby's chin and made her look up.

"It's dead now," she repeated. She looked down, into her daughter's eyes, and Abby realized that her mother didn't look scared. Instead she looked tired and solemn and resolved. "It's dead," her mother repeated.

Abby took a deep breath and nodded. Her heart slowed

just a bit. Looking at her mother's face made her feel a glimmer of calm.

"Go inside and fetch your brother," her mother told her. "Have a cookie. Everything is fine now. And the Johnsons will be here soon."

Abby nodded and scurried back into the house. The kitchen was bright and spotless just like it always was. It smelled of pot roast and baked carrots. The dishes were all laid out neatly on the counter, aluminum foil wrapped over them to keep the heat in. Abby grabbed a cookie from the jar by the fridge and stared at it. She didn't think she could eat it. She stuffed it into her dress pocket and ran into the living room, stumbling to a stop next to the squishy recliner her brother was usually found in. He was playing a video game and didn't look up at her.

"Mom's outside," she blurted, breathless all over again. She shifted uncomfortably from one foot to the other.

Her brother paused the game and looked at her. "And?" he asked, sounding bored. He was only three years ahead of Abby's nine, but thought himself far superior.

"She wants you," Abby told him. "One of those things from the news was out there."

Her brother frowned at her. Abby was clutching the front of her dress in both hands. She realized and tried to smooth the dress out, but she had already wrinkled it. She put her hand in her pocket. She'd broken her cookie and now had nothing but dust and crumbs. Her brother nodded and got up from the couch. He slipped on his dress shoes and walked past her, patting her head as he went. Abby swatted his hand away.

She counted to five and then crept to the back door. She peeked through the curtain at her mother and brother. Her mother and brother both had thick garden gloves on and were dragging the thing to the fire pit. Her mother disappeared into the shed briefly and returned with a red can of gasoline. Abby watched as her mother poured all the gasoline into the fire pit, shaking it to get the last drops out. She handed a book of matches to her brother and he lit a match. They both stepped back as her brother dropped it.

Abby blinked at the bright light as the fire ravenously caught. It flashed white several times, then quickly dimmed to a dark blue. The flames crept along the body searchingly. Her mother and brother stood side by side, silhouetted against the flames. He reached for their mother's hand.

The doorbell rang, and Abby jumped. She glanced at the clock. Six thirty. The Johnsons. They were always on time.

She ran to the front door and peeked through the window on the side. Mr. Johnson was standing there, looking somehow bored and impatient at the same time, arms crossed. Mrs. Johnson was smiling into a compact and reapplying her lipstick. It was dark red and made her mouth look bloody and ragged.

Abby opened the door a crack.

"Can I help you?" she asked. She worried that if she let them in her mother and brother wouldn't be done in the backyard yet. That would lead to questions Abby wasn't sure how to answer.

"Abby!" Mr. Johnson declared. "We're here for dinner. Surely you know? Let us in, little girl." He leaned toward the crack in the door and lowered his voice. "They say it's not safe to linger in the dark." He laughed a little 'oof' of a laugh and shook his head ironically at this last bit, as though he thought it to be nonsense. Mrs. Johnson laughed along with him, a quiet chirrupy laugh, and flicked her hair over one shoulder.

Abby opened the door. "Well, if you really want to," she said. She stood aside and let them in. Mr. Johnson shrugged off his overcoat and held it out to Abby.

"Well, where's your mother at?" he asked. Abby hung his coat on the coat rack and held her hand out for Mrs. Johnson's long fur coat. Mrs. Johnson sneered at her and hugged her coat tighter. She reeked of perfume. Abby watched, transfixed, as she took out her lipstick and began reapplying it once more. Not even bothering to look in her compact, Mrs. Johnson ran the lipstick around and around her mouth. The color was beginning to bleed past her lips. She stared at Abby with cold, dark eyes. Abby felt lightheaded all over again. Mrs. Johnson's perfume was so strong. And there was something else. Some other smell.

"Don't mind Linda, Abby. She's been cold all day," Mr. Johnson told her. He put a hand on his wife's back and they walked down the hallway and into the dining room. Abby trailed behind.

"Where's your mother, Abby?" Mr. Johnson asked once more.

"She's busy right now," Abby said.

"Well, can you let her know we're here?" he asked her. He checked his watch and huffed quietly. "Not even ready," he muttered to himself.

"Sure. Be right back." Abby turned to go through the kitchen door when something caught her eye. Mrs. Johnson's mouth looked lopsided. It was hanging to one side like a ragged tear across her face. Abby was sure it hadn't looked that way when they'd come in. Mr. Johnson didn't appear to have noticed, but then again, he rarely seemed to notice much about his wife. He was comparing the time on his watch to the clock on the wall. He shook his head, pulled the clock off the wall, and began to fiddle with the back of it. Mrs. Johnson's head turned sharply as she caught Abby's stare. She reached up and touched her mouth, then pushed it back into place. She smiled. No. She didn't smile. Mrs. Johnson showed Abby her teeth. They were smeared and globbed with her red lipstick. Abby turned on her heel and ran to the kitchen door. She flung it open and darted across the yard, her chest feeling as though it were being squeezed.

Her mother and brother were pouring buckets of water on the ashes in the fire pit. The smoke stank horribly.

"Mom! They're here!" Abby gasped as some of the smoke blew in her eyes. They immediately began to sting and water.

"Right on time." Her mother's face was grim. "I think that's enough, Dylan." Abby's brother put the bucket down and followed their mother toward the house.

"Mom!" Abby whispered, tugging on her mother's elbow. "Mom, Mrs. Johnson!" They crossed the threshold into the kitchen.

"What, Abby?" Her mother shook her off her arm as she poured more sauce onto the pot roast.

"Mrs. Johnson. She's weird!" Abby hissed. She felt panicked; she wasn't saying it right. Her heart was beating so fast. She took a deep breath.

"She's always been a little weird, honey," her mother whispered back. She gestured to her brother to carry the pot roast and picked up the bowl of salad.

"But she's wrong! She's wrong!" Abby looked at her mother with pleading eyes. She didn't know how to say it. She wasn't even sure what was happening, but she knew Mrs. Johnson was no longer Mrs. Johnson.

"What?" Abby's mother cupped her chin and studied her face for the second time that day. "What do you mean?"

Just then Mr. Johnson flung open the kitchen door. "Margaret! We're starving. Don't mind feeding us, do you?" He laughed at his own joke.

"Of course not," Abby's mother trilled.

Abby followed her mother and brother into the dining room, bobbing about nervously. Abby tugged at her mother's elbow again.

"Go sit, Abby." Her mother sounded a bit cross.

Abby shuffled toward the table and sat down in her normal spot with her back to the kitchen door. Her brother sat on her right, at one the end of the table. Mr. Johnson had placed himself at the other end. Mrs. Johnson came and sat down on Abby's left. Mrs. Johnson smiled at her again and brushed the back of Abby's hand with her fingertips, scratching her with one long red nail. Abby jerked her hand away and looked at Mr. Johnson, but he was busy talking to Abby's mother, who was starting to carve the pot roast.

"I've fixed your clock there, Margaret. It was four minutes slow."

"Why thank you, Harold." Abby's mother was all politeness and good cheer.

"Do you believe any of this nonsense they're plastering all over the news these days, Margaret?" Mr. Johnson leaned back in his chair, clearly in his element—talking someone's ear off. "They have their own land, their own space. We've lived peacefully side by side for decades. I mean, this is the twenty third century for crying out loud. We've gotten along for almost a hundred years. Why would they attack us now? And all this nonsense about them eating us and then wearing us like skins. It's all politics and propaganda if you ask me."

A strange growling sound emanated from Mrs. Johnson. Everyone turned to look at her. She smiled and patted her stomach. Mr. Johnson laughed heartily. Abby froze, afraid to move.

"Why indeed," her mother murmured.

Abby watched as her mother held Mrs. Johnson's gaze. Mrs. Johnson's smile widened. She showed more of her teeth, smeared with red. Abby's mother smiled calmly back.

"If you wouldn't mind excusing me just one moment," Abby's mother said. "I've forgotten the carrots." She passed behind Abby and into the kitchen.

Mr. Johnson continued yammering this time in Dylan's direction. Abby stared in horror as Mrs. Johnson scratched at her cheek. Her skin moved unnaturally, as though it were not quite attached. Abby sat, frozen and gripped her steak knife as Mrs. Johnson scratched at her neck, her skin sliding about. Mrs. Johnson noticed Abby's attention and smiled, showing her red, red teeth. She reached out and gently stroked Abby's hand. Abby yanked her hand away and caught another whiff of Mrs. Johnson's perfume along with the something else she thought she had smelled earlier. It was something dead.

"Margaret!" Mr. Johnson spluttered. "What in the world?!"

Abby jerked her head forward and saw her mother's shadow on the wall. She had the axe raised.

**About the Author**

Ashley Libey received her Bachelor's in English Literature from Western Washington University in 2011. She worked briefly as an editorial assistant for a book reviewer and holds a deep, dark understanding of the slush pile. She enjoys reading works from all genres (apart from romance, ew) and currently mediates an online writing group. Ashley can usually be found writing, dancing tango, or crocheting yet another blanket.

# CAJOLED

BRONTË PEARSON

I awoke to a sore back, planked across a freezing metal table. My hands and feet were bound by what felt like bungee cords, and I could feel the cool fingers of the air around me drift over most parts of my skin.

I screamed. The sound seemed to only make it about ten feet in diameter before ricocheting back at me. The room around me was dark, but as my eyes adjusted, I could just barely make out the form of a tool bench to my right.

I screamed again, but it seemed to get lost in the walls. My eyes flooded and my breathing quickened as I panicked beneath my restraints. My tears uncomfortably pooled around my mouth, and all I could taste was salt.

I reminded myself that crying and panicking was not going to get me out of here. I tried to train my breathing to slow into a steady pace and blinked my tears away. Once my eyes were clear, I looked down at my cold, shaking body and realized I was dressed in the schoolgirl lingerie I had bought from Spencer's.

I started convulsing. I couldn't control myself. I had no choice but to panic. The longer I struggled, the more my forehead pulsated and stung. I thought of Jordan. I wondered what he was doing right now. I wondered if anyone would tell him I was missing. I imagined he would shrug it off and think I was being overly emotional and had taken off. To him, my sensitivity was my greatest fault. But, perhaps, he would feel differently. Perhaps, he would be the one who found me. My stomach churned at the thought.

I heard a door open in the distance, following by a low but powerful hum that echoed through the walls. I recognized the voice behind the hum, and everything became clearer. I held my breath until I couldn't any longer. I pictured my last breaths floating through the air and circulating around the world. I thought about how they would, someday, find themselves conveniently brushing Jordan's cheek on some breezy afternoon, and a piece of me would touch him one last time, even if he never knew.

The world around me began to pixelate into clouded figures, and my eyes began to slouch, until a white suit cuff brushed my cheek and snapped everything into focus.

***

I should have known better than to go into Spencer's. Deadpool merchandise was fucking *everywhere.* Jordan loved Deadpool. It was the last thing in the world I needed, but I ventured into the dim storefront anyway. I realized I was turning into my mother, shopping as a means of therapy. "Money can't fix everything" was a load of bullshit, and I was willing to do whatever it took to get my mind off him.

Deadpool's face taunted me in various forms from the fronts of shirts, coffee mugs, socks, belts, hats, and the like. I spotted a Deadpool wallet similar to the one I had gotten him just a few weeks ago for his birthday. He had smiled but didn't thank me. He called off our engagement the next day.

"How's it going? Is there anything I can help you find today?" the cashier shouted over the music. Her hair stood in peaks on her pink head. It perfectly depicted the rise and fall of the roaring heavy metal.

"I'm good. Thanks," I replied.

"Let me know if you need anything," she said, her nose ring jiggling between her nostrils as she smiled her fake I-have-to-smile-because-I-work-here grin. I nodded.

The further I walked into the store, the less Deadpool haunted me. T-shirts with desperate attempts at shock appeal hung in pleated lines, its letters in garish colors and fonts. I tried to picture someone who wasn't a total douchebag wearing them, but it was impossible. Almost as if on cue, a kid with a black-dyed Mohawk rounded the corner and stopped in front of a shirt that had its text turned sideways which read, "IF YOU TURN YOUR

HEAD TO READ THIS YOU OWE ME A BLOW JOB." He thought it was hilarious and pulled it from the rack. I rolled my eyes and continued walking.

Pink lights illuminated the back of the store where the "adult" items were housed. I felt slightly repulsed by some of the items along the shelves, but a part of me wanted to splurge on lingerie and sex toys just for the fact that it was totally out of my character.

The pain from our breakup had made me want to rebel in every way possible. The day he moved out, I cried until no tears were left, then spontaneously drove to the nearest tattoo parlor at 9:00 that night. I now have a random lighthouse on my ribcage. It hurt like hell.

I let my fingers graze over the lacy panties and eyed the sexy schoolgirl lingerie set near me. I pictured myself in it, my sides poking out a bit too far and my butt sagging a little too low for it to look as good as it did on the model in the cover photo. I could buy it and take seductive pictures of myself in it, posing in angles that made me look sexier than I really was, and then post them on a blogging site like Tumblr under a sexy pseudonym.

I grabbed a size nine from the shelf.

I continued to walk through the maze of naughty toys. I even stopped to sniff the Sweet Licks warming red velvet cupcake flavored massage lotion. It didn't smell much like red velvet cupcakes.

The longer I waded through the pink-lit cavern, the more I started to feel disgusted with myself. I also thought about how Jordan would probably have wanted to keep me longer if I'd shopped here more. I drifted over to the girl with the screaming hair and laid my schoolgirl outfit on the counter. She looked at me, surveying my blotchy skin and greasy hair. I hadn't worn a drop of makeup or bothered to shower in days.

She gave me the total, and I silently paid her, and then stuffed the sack into the large JC Penney's bag I had been lugging around with me.

The florescent lights stung my eyes as they adjusted to the real world, and a melting pot of voices erupted around me as I exited the store. One voice piled on another, and it sounded as if every person in Oklahoma City was in this one part of the mall. I suddenly felt overwhelmed and couldn't wait to leave.

I strolled past blurs of families, couples, and teenaged cliques. I kept my eyes fixed on the linoleum and tried to watch out for nearby feet and wheels. I could just see the exit doors when a man in a suit stepped out from behind an island in the aisle.

"Good afternoon, ma'am! Would you like to try Billotrix's new long-lasting 24-hour perfume?"

"Oh, no, thank you." I tried not to make eye contact as I continued to walk, but he cut in front of me.

"You don't have to buy any today. Just try a spray and notice how long our fabulous formula lasts. I promise, it will have you coming back for a bottle! We have a deal going on right now for 25% off. If you'll try it for me today and decide you like it, I will give you an extra 10% off. How does that sound?" He flashed his best salesman smile, his teeth in straight, immaculate rows that sparkled under the intense mall lighting.

His persistence was frustrating, and his charisma reminded me of Jordan, which only frustrated me more. I was eager to get out of the mall. I stood for a second then nodded. "Okay, alright. Go ahead."

"Excellent!" He pulled a cylindrical glass bottle from his suit jacket's pocket and demonstrated how I should hold out my wrist.

I held my wrist out, still attempting to avoid eye contact. The man spritzed my wrist twice.

"Now rub your wrists together and take a whiff! Notice the blend of floral scents. It's made with real essential oils that persist all day long."

I sniffed my wrists. I had to admit, the perfume was rather pleasing. "This is really nice," I said. "I may just be back."

"Fabulous! I hope to see you back here soon! Have a wonderful rest of the afternoon." He bowed in my direction as if I was worthy of the utmost praise for actually liking his product. Mall salespeople were always a bit too over the top for my taste, but it made me feel kind of nice.

I finally escaped the mall and embraced the warm gust that cuddled against my skin in contrast to the chilliness I had endured for the past hour and a half I'd spent shopping.

I slithered through the maze of cars that sprinkled the parking lot. I couldn't remember exactly which row I had parked in, but I figured I would get there eventually. After a few moments, my head started to pound, so I knew I had to think harder about where the car was parked. Finally, I saw the red Hyundai a few rows down. I powerwalked in its direction until my vision began to blur, and I felt a sudden pang of nausea. I realized I hadn't eaten in several hours and figured I could have been experiencing a low blood sugar episode, as I did on occasion.

I finally reached the car. I fumbled in my purse for the keys, but I found my dexterity was off. My hands felt like they had been caked in plaster and hardened into a cast. My vision continued to blur, and my head continued to roar. I stumbled into the trunk of the car to maintain my balance, but it wasn't enough to resist the force of gravity. I felt the asphalt bite my face, and then everything disappeared.

***

His hands were soft and strong, just as they had been when I had shaken his hand earlier in the day. As his skin skated along my face, my body felt as if it was sprouting inward-facing spines, piercing every inch of my body. Suddenly, his hands slapped over my mouth, pushing my head harshly into the metal beneath me, and he smothered my nose with a damp washcloth. I became overwhelmed by the floral undertones of the perfume I had enjoyed so well merely hours ago. My body relaxed, and the screeching of an electric drill was the last thing I heard as I melted into the blackness.

## About the Author

Brontë Pearson is a Science Writing Master's student at Johns Hopkins University, and a recent graduate of the University of Arkansas at Monticello in Creative Writing. Brontë enjoys writing both fiction and poetry and has previously published both genres in journals such as *Black Mirror Magazine, Linden Avenue Literary Journal, 805 Lit + Art Magazine*, and others.

Brontë's electronic portfolio can be found at http://bronteelise.wix.com/brontepearson.

# A MOTHER'S LOVE

MICAH CASTLE

The small fires burning around our clearing blanketed everything in a warm glow. I stood outside and watched as mother carved the family symbol into one of the many trees surrounding our home.

With a crudely made knife she made a jagged circle into the oak's body, then striking, made several lines crossing through. Her ragged white gown jerked with her movements and her haggard hair kept sticking to her face. Once she was done she came near and pulled me close. Her arms wrapped around my child body like the limbs of the trees, thin, strong, sturdy. I could smell the sweat on her this close.

"Are you ready to pray, dear?"

I nodded. In unison we spoke the Prayer and swayed with the words.

"O' forest, trees, and Mother,

"Give us peace, protection from all others;

"O' Mother who is everything pure around our home,

"Never let harm come to us, not flesh, nor bone;

"O' Mother on this dawn of Halloween, we worship,

"For love, for safeguard, for a year of no hardship."

We finished, then bowed our heads and silently thanked Mother. My mother turned me and pushed me towards to the rickety home. After she had put out the small fires with handfuls of dirt and sand, she came inside. She shut the door and tied the rope around a hook to keep it closed throughout the night.

Underneath a thin sheet she cradled me, held me close to her bosom, whispered sweet things into my ears into the lull of sleep enveloped me and I drifted off. I still felt her warmth in the nothingness and prayed to anyone who could hear my thoughts for it to never end.

At midnight on every Halloween we prayed to Her, gave thanks to Her and She, I believed, gave me mother, gave me her love and heat, gave me the food she brought from the forest, gave me the logs she cuts for fires — She gave me everything I knew and loved.

The treetops turned to autumnal colors: yellows, oranges, reds and browns. The leaves fell and drifted down from the branches and sat onto the slowly dying grass. The smell of the river and dying leaves were thick in the cold air. I sat on the small step up of our home, wrapped in a thin sheet, and watched as mother cut logs. The rusted axe we found underneath the dirt came down with a powerful *thunk* as it cut through another slab of wood.

Sweat covered my mother, her gown stuck to her body revealing her breasts and abdomen. I could smell what was in between her legs from where I sat, but she could smell mine too. It was Wednesday, and bathing day was not until Friday. We kept track of days by marking an X in the dirt, and we kept time by a wristwatch we found on the river's shore. Once I asked mother how long had it been since I was born, and she did not remember; another time, I asked her how long had it been since she came to the forest, with father, she did not remember; and I asked her lastly where father went, she said she did not remember. I wanted to ask more, like where she learned the words she taught me or how she learned to build the traps that caught our food, but her mind was like the river, always flowing away.

The sudden sound of the axe slamming into the cutting log echoed throughout the still forest, filled it up for a brief moment like lightning in a stormy sky. Then, subtle, the sound of leaves crackling, twigs and branches snapping, shot through the air.

Before the man and boy came into our clearing, mother had stood before me, axe raised in one hand. From where I sat I could see her pale, hairy legs and dirt caked heels.

The man wore bright orange over green, brown and black clothes; an oily, grizzly, beard covered most of his face; his dirtied boots sunk into the leaves and grass as he walked. A firearm was slung over his shoulder. The boy behind him kept close but not near enough to bump into the man, and wore the same clothes, though they seemed cleaner.

"Looks like you might need a man's help," the man said, grinning, his words spoken with a drawl. I looked passed my mother and saw his eyes move over her body, focus on her breasts and the part in between her legs. He could smell it too.

"Leave our clearing!" My mother shouted, tightening her grip on the axe handle, the sinewy muscles on her forearms tightened underneath her pasty skin.

"Don't be like that miss, I'm just offering some help. I help you," he said, licking his lips, "then you can help me."

"I need no help! Leave our home!"

The man laughed, then spat blackened saliva. "Fine be that way, bitch." He said, then began walking back into the forest. "C'mon boy, let's leave. They're not worth our time, they're worth no one's time."

The boy stood idly as the man neared the edge of the clearing. His big blue eyes were locked onto me. Before he could raise his hand, the man gripped his arm and pulled him away.

"Leave those whores alone." He whispered, seething. "Their cunts aren't worth it, no matter how good they smell."

Then they were gone. The sound of breaking twigs and rustling leaves soon left, too. The silence returned, and mother resumed chopping wood.

***

I did not know how long five years was, but I was much taller and older now. It was many, many days after mother passed. I woke up one morning to find her grasp cold, her arms and muscles tough and hard; her chest unmoving; her wide, glossy eyes seemed to stare into my soul; her frail mouth open in a permanent gasp. The smell of shit filled the house and I found the back of her gown stained brown.

For the rest of the day I sat in the corner, my knees

drawn to my chest and my hair over my face, and cried.

The next day I went out behind the house and dug a hole with my hands. I washed myself in the cold river that night, as if cleansing myself would prepare me for the task coming.

As the sun peeked over the horizon, the sky turned a warm yellow. I took my mother by her ankles and dragged her to the door, a streak of dried filth left behind. By lifting her and placing her onto my shoulder, I carried her out to the hole behind the house. Carefully I knelt and placed her inside. With handfuls of dirt softened by the tears that started days ago, I buried her. The earth took her into its womb and what was left of her, left of her soul, drifted into Mother.

The following and every day after, I did the duties mother showed me how to do. I emptied the traps of what food was caught, I chopped logs and made firewood, I placed bundles of twigs and sticks around our — my — clearing, and I sharpened the knife on the rocks near the river as the tied bucket filled with water.

I, then, waited as the heat swelled inside the house and filled the air around my clearing with moisture. I waited as rain fell hard, leaking through the roof and walls, filling the soil until everything was one large puddle. I waited until the breeze had cooled and the leaves began to change colors.

It was the eve of Halloween. I prepared the kindling and started the fires around the clearing, found a trunk of a tree to carve to give thanks to Mother, then waited on the step of home until it was nearing the dawn of Halloween.

I must have fallen asleep, because when I awoke I was no longer outside but on the floor of the house. The back of my head throbbed. My gown was up and there was a sudden, sharp pain shooting up from between my legs. It was night and I couldn't see but I heard grunts and moans and smelt the stench of sweat and piss. I felt breath, hot and heavy against my chest. In between my legs something thrusted into me.

I opened my eyes to see bright blue ones looking at me. The boy was now the man. He leaned forward, placed his rancid mouth to my ear and spoke softly,

"You like that? Like your cunt filled? I bet your mom wished she could've had my dad, but no, she had to be a bitch."

Then he gritted his teeth and thrusted harder into me. My pelvis burned and felt like it was going to break. Blood seeped in between him and me, puddling underneath my backside. I was beyond moving, beyond thinking or escaping. Idly I laid like a sack of meat as he used me.

The wristwatch was on the floor, its face to me. The warm glow of the fires faintly came in through the open door. I saw it was two minutes to midnight, to the dawn of Halloween.

"I must go," I said as tears streamed over my face. "I must pray to Mother."

"You're not goin anywhere bitch. Once I'm done with you, I'mma bring my buddies around."

"No! I must go! Pl—"

"Shut up!" He shouted and punched me in the face. The back of my head hit against the floorboards and I felt blood trickle out of me. Then his hand was inside my mouth, gagging me.

I screamed, though all that came out was muffled noises. I watched the hand of the clock tick, tick, tick until it was the dawn of Halloween.

He groaned loudly, closing his eyes and his chapped, oily lips curled into a smile. His body trembled. A warm liquid filled me, intertwining with blood.

"You like that? I bet you do. All women do, they love a good fuckin' — love to get filled up, ain't that right?"

He released me and stood, zipped up his pants. I laid there staring at the watch. In-between my legs throbbed and pulsated with a sharp pain I had never felt before, never wanted to feel, and my legs were like the broken branches I use for kindling.

"That it? All you gonna do, bitch, lay there?" He said, kicking my feet. "Get up."

I could not move, even if I wanted to.

"Get up!" He kicked my legs.

"Fine!" He shouted after a moment. "If you won't get up, I'll make you."

The man grabbed my waist and picked me over his shoulder. He carried me out into the clearing and put me on the ground. He whistled, and I heard rustling in the trees. More men came out from the shadows of the forest. More men with their greasy faces that glistened above the glow of the fires.

"Here she is boys! Have at her!" He said, grinning.

As I made the sign in the grass, I spoke the prayer under my breath.

"O' forest, trees, and Mother,

"Give us peace, protection from all others;"

The men neared me, undoing their pants and taking off their clothes.

"O' Mother who is everything pure around our home,

"Never let harm come to us, not flesh, nor bone;"

Some had knives, others had rusty poles that were caked with dirt and dried blood.

"O' Mother on this dawn of Halloween, we worship,

"For love, for safeguard, for a year of no hardship."

***

Darkness engulfed the clearing. I stared at the sign in the grass and muttered the prayers over and over again. The fires went out and a cold wind whipped through the area, chilling my flesh and raising goose bumps. I heard the man walk around, heard him ask, "What the hell is going on? Why'd the fires go out?"

Then one by one, there were screams. Men were pulled back into the forest, thrown against the trees, broken against the rocky shore of the river. They were flung into the air and dragged down into the soil. They were ripped and stretched against the tree-tops like spider webs. Although I could not see this in the dark, I saw it in my mind.

Each one destroyed by Mother, each one punished for interrupting Her prayer. The boy that was now a man grabbed me and lifted me up. Like a doll I never had, I dangled in his grip.

"What'd you do? What the fuck is going on!"

He could not see it, but I smiled.

Then he released me. I heard his cries and screams as his body vanished into the depths of Mother's gloom.

Silence swelled and filled everything. Not an owl hooted, not a cricket chirped; even the river seemed frozen. The breeze ceased. The darkness swelled and sucked into itself, forming a ball of black above me. Flames blossomed from the fires as I sat in the center of the clearing, looking up.

The ball billowed, and tendrils slithered out, twisting, turning, weaving in the air like a tapestry being made. It formed arms and legs, a body and a head — then a face.

It was my mother and Mother, standing a foot away. Their features were intertwined and overlapping. They were young and beautiful, and they smiled and stretched their arms out.

I ran to them, crying and smiling. They embraced me with their misty, warm arms, and I felt my mother's love once more.

**About the Author**

Micah Castle is a person who writes short horror/weird fiction. His stories have been published via *Shoggoth.net*, *Crimson Streets*, and *Horror Bites Magazine*. He has two books currently out, *The Stone Man and Other Weird Tales* and *Who*

*Spoke on the Other Side.*

While away from the keyboard, he enjoys aimlessly hiking through the woods, playing with his animals, and can typically be found reading a book somewhere in his home.

You can follow Micah and find all the latest news about him the following locations:

Twitter @Micah_Castle
www.facebook.com/TheMicahCastle
www.micahcastle.com

# PROVIDENT JUSTICE

CARRIE CONNEL-GRIPP

Fresh start. New life. Second chance. The litany wound its way through Robin Campbell's brain. A new home in another state. A chance for the past to be buried for a long time. Robin looked at his sixteen-year-old son's glowering image in the rear-view mirror. It had been a terrible year for Peter. Jennifer died early in January taking their eleven-year-old daughter Anna with her. The wreckage was unrecognizable and dental records were used to identify the bodies.

Then Peter was accused of stealing from another student; next a teacher. His alibis never panned out. On July 6$^{th}$, he opened the front door to confront two police officers on the front porch. Between them, his son looked at him in silent defiance. Not for the first time, Peter feigned listening while Robin talked about reform or military. When asked if he had anything to say for himself, Peter replied, "I should have gone with Mom."

Robin was losing touch. When the position was posted for Wanakanda, he walked straight into his boss's office and said, "I want that job."

***

Wanakanda, population 368. Robin stopped at the first light to check the map. Two more lights, then right, down half a block: 51 Settlers Drive. For ten-thirty on a Friday night, the town looked very quiet and dark, few streetlights lit. Robin continued down the main street and stopped at the next red light. Along the left side of the street, there were several blocks of stores like in any small town. On the opposite side, other than the faint outline of one small building, there was only blackness. Just before the light turned green, a wild moan issued from the dark.

"What the hell was that," said Peter, sitting forward in the backseat.

"Oh, you're awake. We'll be at our new home soon," said Robin, pulling away from the four-corners. He double-checked the map and stopped at the red light at Settlers Drive. He turned right. A police siren split the silence. Robin stopped the car and rolled down the window.

A deep booming voice forced its way into the car. "Don't you realize you can go to jail for doing that, Mister?"

"Uh, no, sorry, Officer...," He looked at the nametag pinned to the man's shirt, "Burton. I didn't realize it was against law here."

An old-style officer's hat, over moon face, thrust through the opening. "You're new in town."

"Yes, sir. We're just moving into the house at 51," Robin looked around.

The officer looked to see where Robin was pointing and shrugged his shoulders. "I'll let you off this time. First thing tomorrow, you pick up the *Book of Laws* at the town clerk's office. You don't want to be spending a night in jail 'cause of something stupid."

"No, sir. I'll do that before." Robin smiled at the man.

"You better get inside." The officer looked at his watch. "You're thirteen minutes away from curfew." The officer walked back to his car.

"Curfew! Fuck, Dad, what've you gotten us into?"

"Don't swear, Peter."

The tires scrunched on the gravel drive and they got out. "Just grab your suitcase. We'll get the rest in the morning," said Robin, as he fumbled for the house key.

Creaking open, the door released a musty sigh. Robin searched for the light switch, his hand crashing through cobwebs. The sudden brightness revealed avocado shag and a chocolate chaise lounge.

"Shit! I thought your company had money," sneered Peter.

Robin glared at him. "I think this place was forgotten when we bought out the plant. Go open the back door so we can air it out." He stepped over the threshold, trying not to breathe deeply. Walking through each room, he first flicked on the light and opened the window. Peter met him back in the living room.

"It's gonna take a year to get rid of this stench."

"Hrumph," came from the front door.

"Officer Burton," said a surprised Robin. "What can I do for you?"

"Curfew's past. Lights out. Get the *Book of Laws* tomorrow. Read it!" The officer turned and slipped into the darkness. "Lights out!" accosted them from the street.

Robin shook himself. "You heard him. Let's get those lights off."

Peter looked at him strangely.

"Now!"

Peter headed for the back of the house as his father turned off the lights in the front. Slamming into Robin in the hall, Peter said, "Okay, how are we supposed to find our bedrooms? And I'm hungry."

Robin grabbed his son's shoulder with one hand and eased him through the doorway on the right, just discernible in the near darkness.

"Here's your room. Go to sleep. There isn't any food in the house."

Robin heard mumbling as he entered his own room on the left. "Peter, we're both tired. Go to sleep." He heard the twin bed creak as Peter lay down.

***

Waking slowly from a numbing sleep, Robin heard pounding.

"Dad, who the fuck is it?" Peter stumbled down the hall and met Robin at the front door. Robin pulled the wooden slab open. A man with a beatific face and premature grey hair, met them with a "Halloo, neighbor! Gotta make hay while the sun shines."

"Good morning," said Robin hesitantly.

"Yeah, sure, it's always a good one. I'm Rashad, from across the street. It's already seven-thirty. You got lots to do today. Better get started."

Robin looked at his new acquaintance strangely. "Yeah. We met with a police officer last night who said something about a book of laws?"

"I've been appointed by the council to get you oriented. Meetings are set up. You have thirty minutes before the first one. I'll come back in twenty." Rashad walked quickly down the sidewalk.

Peter poked his father in the side making him jump. "I'd really like to know what the hell's wrong with this town," he said, adolescent voice cracking.

Robin glared at him. "I'm going to get ready. Go out to the car and bring in the box with the coffeemaker in it." He heard a muffled "Get it yourself, dickweed," before the front door slammed.

***

Peter had the car partially unloaded when Robin emerged refreshed, dressed in shirt, tie and casual pants.

"Didn't find the coffee, yet," said Peter. "Seems like there's a few other things missing, too."

"Like what?"

Before Peter could answer, Rashad called from the other side of the street. "Time to go. We'll take my car."

Robin instructed Peter to finish unpacking and get a start on cleaning the house. Peter watched the car pull away and turn the corner towards the center of town. As his eyes swept over the neighborhood, he noticed the entire street was devoid of grass.

***

"Do you work at the plant?" asked Robin.

"Sure, everyone does, except those who work in the

town clerk's office, or who run the stores, and the police officers and the minister. Wanakanda probably wouldn't exist without the plant." Rashad turned onto a side street and stopping by a large, grey brick building. He led the way up the steps into an open room with an old-fashioned office desk behind a counter.

"Bill," called Rashad. A thin, short man wearing a bow tie stuck his head out of a door in the back.

"I'll be right out," he called back. "Just take a seat."

Rashad turned to Robin and gestured to a row of black vinyl chairs along one wall. "You sit, wait for Bill. I've got an errand to run. I'll come back to get you and we'll go over to the plant." He went out the door whistling.

Robin paced the room, looking at the photos on the walls.

"Did I say 'take a seat'?" asked Bill from behind the counter.

"Yes, you did."

"I thought so," he said. "What is it I can help you with?"

"I was instructed to get the books of laws," said Robin, sheepishly. "I'm new in town. Taking over management of the plant."

"Ah, you're the one." Bill reached, drew out a small book. It was the size of a five-by-seven inch picture frame and approximately half an inch thick. The black leather cover reminded Robin of his wife's old family bible, complete with gold embossed letters that proclaimed it as *The Book of Laws of Wanakanda.* Robin reached for the book, but Bill snatched it away, sliding a piece of paper across the counter with his other hand.

"Sign this release form first."

Robin filled it out and held it up in front of him. "I'll trade you," he joked.

Bill took the sheet of paper between thumb and forefinger. Before handing over the book, he said, "Don't lose it. You can go to jail for something that stupid, you know." With an icy tone, he added, "Take a seat while you wait for Rashad."

"Yeah, sure." Robin sat and thumbed through the first few pages of the book, where he discovered it was first published in 1858.

***

"You'll have to give those up," said a voice from behind Peter. He jerked his head to look around, knocking it against the edge of the upraised rear door of the station wagon.

"Not on your life," he said around the cigarette between his lips. "I'm Peter."

"Jessie." She was a small girl, about fifteen years old, wearing a yellow sundress and sandals. Her hair, the palest blonde Peter had ever seen, was tied back in a loose ponytail. "You won't find any in town."

Peter took a deep pull on his smoke and flicked it under the wheels of the car. "I brought a whole carton with me. I just can't find it."

"Not surprising. Someone probably went through your car and took out all the contraband. Can I help?" Jessie grabbed a small box and headed to the house.

Peter hoisted another to his shoulder and followed her. "Did you see someone?"

"Curfew. I was asleep." Jessie put down her box in the living room.

"Guess that would explain the missing coffee beans and bottle of whiskey. Dad'll be pissed about those." Peter dropped his box on the floor beside the other one, reached into his shirt pocket and withdrew the pack of cigarettes. "Shit. Only half a pack left."

Jessie crinkled her nose in distaste at Peter's colorful language. She looked about the room, noting the dated décor. "I can help you clean the place up if you like."

"Oh, well, you could help me finish unpacking the car.

I'll get to the cleaning later." Jessie nodded and they returned outside.

"There'll be lots of things you'll have to get used to. First day at school will be a shock."

"Yeah? I came from a school with zero tolerance."

"Here, it's subzero tolerance."

"What do you mean by that?"

"You can't even have a criminal thought."

"What, thought police? We're a long way from *1984*."

Jessie looked puzzled. "What does 1984 have to do with anything? I wasn't even born then."

"*1984*? Book by George Orwell? Movie starring John Hurt? You never heard of it?"

Jessie shook her head.

"Come back inside. I've got a copy." Peter dug into a box just inside the front door. "Hey, my books have been rifled through. There's no *1984*, no *Catcher in the Rye*, lots of others are missing too. Somebody's head is gonna roll."

"There's nothing you can do about it."

"That's my property. No one has the right to take my stuff!"

***

"Come on, Peter," shouted Robin. "The invitation was for two o'clock sharp!"

Sauntering down the hall, Peter glared at his father. "I don't see why I have to go," he whined.

"Because the invitation was for both of us and it'll give you a chance to meet people your own age before you get to school tomorrow.

"Great," mumbled Peter as he shut the door behind them.

They walked across the street to Rashad's house. As instructed, Robin led Peter around to the garden gate and into the backyard. Several people were already there and turned to look as they came around the corner of the house. Rashad called Robin over to the barbecue and introduced him to several of the men he hadn't met yet, explaining each of their roles at the plant. Peter saw Jessie and joined her by the side of the pool. Jessie's mother, Nina, brought Peter a glass of lemonade and asked what he thought of Wanakanda.

"Well, it's a much smaller town than where we lived before," he said with a small shrug.

"You're going to really like it here. I can sense that you'll fit in." Nina echoed the shrug and pushed her dark brown shoulder length hair behind her ears. "It can be difficult though, if you weren't born here." She walked away to join the other women around the picnic table.

"How difficult can it be?" asked Peter.

"Don't know. I was born here." Jessie turned her attention to a group of young people just arriving. "All of them were born here too."

A smart looking boy with wire-framed glasses, led the group to poolside. "Hey, Jessie. Who's your new friend?"

"Everybody, this is Peter. He just moved across the street to number 51. This is Jimmy, Patricia, Rob, Greg and Dawn." Peter thought it was strange that all his new companions had the same pale blond hair as Jessie.

After polite small talk about school, music and other interests, Jimmy stripped off his shirt and said, "Anyone actually going to swim at this pool party, or what?" He ran and performed a cannonball, splashing the others which set them all off, diving and splashing. Peter was the last to join them.

Watching his son, Robin was pleased to see Peter making friends and having fun. It had been a long time since he heard his son laugh with such abandon.

***

Later that evening, Robin and Peter sat on the front porch, discussing the events of the last few days.

"You did a good job cleaning the house, Peter. That musty smell is almost gone."

"Yeah, almost, but not quite." After a short silence, Peter said, "I know I put up a fuss when you first told me we were moving, Dad, but I think this was a good thing."

"Thanks, Peter. I hope we'll be able to make a better life for ourselves here."

"It's a bit weird though, don't you think?"

Robin shrugged. "Everyone's incredibly nice, something we're not used to."

"Yeah, there's that. But didn't you notice something funny about the parents today?"

"I don't think so," said Robin, perplexed.

"I tried not to stare, but it was hard."

"Stare at what?"

"At their backs. Almost all of them, the men and women, had scars on their left shoulder."

"Yes, I noticed a few. Rashad had one that looked kinda like an eye."

"I saw one that looked like a fire within a circle. I think that was Jimmy's mother."

"His father had the same one. Well, it's weird all right. It's also late. We both have big days tomorrow. Bedtime."

They went inside and Peter headed for the bathroom to wash up. Robin checked his watch. "Hurry up, son. It's 10:53."

***

Routine set in quickly for Robin and Peter. Robin started work at the plant and, with the help of all the employees, learned the methods of production quickly and instituted new company policies that had been discussed with him prior to the transfer. Everything at the plant ran smoothly and Robin found himself on the production floor helping out more than being in the office.

Robin was happy that Peter quickly settled himself into

the routine of school, doing his homework every night, studying for tests and exams. His best marks were in his morals and ethics course. Peter often went out with friends, always making it home before curfew. Well into the school year, Robin was cooking dinner when he heard the doorbell. He opened the front door and found a familiar scene.

"Why, Peter?" he asked his son. Peter stared at his feet.

"Mr. Campbell. Your son was caught stealing from the variety store at the corner of Smith and Main," said Officer Burton. "Since he was caught red-handed, he will be punished."

"What do you mean 'punished'?" asked Robin. "And who determines what that punishment is?"

"It's the same for all the kids, Mr. Campbell. If you had read the *Book of Laws*, you would know."

"I don't understand. If there was no damage done, couldn't you just give him a warning and let me punish him?"

"I'm taking you both downtown. Please get in the car, Mr. Campbell."

As the car turned from Settlers Drive onto the main street, Robin saw a fire blazing on the vacant side. The police car pulled up behind the crowd that stood watching. It seemed the entire population had turned out as if for an event of great importance. Officer Burton got out of the car and opened the back door to allow Robin and Peter to get out. The town clerk stepped forward to assist in escorting the two to the small building in the middle of the ravaged lot.

"Since the Campbells are the newest members of the community, I will briefly explain to them the purpose and procedure," said Bill. "Mr. Campbell, your son was caught stealing. As his punishment, he will spend one night in the old town jail. Whatever happens to him inside this building, will be for him only. Hopefully, it will assist him in recognizing the error of his ways and he will work to improve himself. As his father, you will willingly accept the consequences." Bill turned to Rashad who stood nearest the building. "Open the door."

Rashad pulled out a skeleton key, released the large padlock and swung the door inwards. Peter struggled as Officer Burton pushed him towards the open door. "What's the big deal about an old building? What's going to happen to me?" asked Peter, his voice cracking.

The police officer pushed Peter inside and slammed the door shut. Rashad replaced the padlock and secured the key in his pocket. People began to move about, setting up lawn chairs and pulling drinks out of coolers.

"We brought a chair for you, Robin. Have a seat. It'll be a long night," said Rashad, who sat with Nina and Jessie.

Robin numbly sat down and accepted the bottle of juice handed to him. He opened his mouth to ask a question, but was shushed by Nina.

"Doesn't help any. Just sit back and relax," said Rashad.

***

The thick, distressed door opened inward without a sound. The townsfolk gasped as Peter stepped into the sunshine. Robin did not recognize him. Everything about his son had been bleached: hair, skin, even his clothing had been drained of color, except for a tint of blue. Robin stood still and waited. After blinking his eyes numerous times, Peter gazed at the crowd. He then stepped toward his father. Stopping three feet from where his father stood, he held out his right hand.

"Take it." His voice had left puberty behind.

Robin hesitated, shocked by his son's appearance. After Peter prompted him a second time, he reached out and grasped the iron bar. He twirled it around in his fingers, examining it. A square of metal had been welded to one end. Inside the square was the image of a severed hand.

"Come to the fire, Mr. Campbell," said Bill.

Robin looked up, incomprehension on his face. Rashad and Officer Burton flanked him, each grabbing an elbow, and directing him toward the flames. Robin shook his head. "This is barbaric. You can't be serious."

Bill took the iron from Robin and shoved the square end into the embers. "You should kneel down," he said. Officer Burton pushed his nightstick into the back of Robin's legs, causing them to bend, and Rashad helped to ease him to the ground.

"This can't be happening," said Robin, looking around at the crowd. He struggled against the police officer's strong hand on his shoulder.

After several minutes, Bill pulled the iron out of the fire; it glowed a soft red. "Not quite hot enough," he said shoving it back into the flames. Several more minutes went by and Bill nodded to Officer Burton.

"Remove your jacket and shirt," the officer said to Robin.

"What? No, I'm not going to do this." Robin attempted to stand. The officer pushed him back down and Rashad grabbed the front of his jacket, undoing the zipper and easing it off his shoulders. The officer then reached down, took hold of the collar of Robin's cotton shirt with both hands and ripped it down the back.

"I promise we'll make this quick," said Bill as he pulled the iron from the fire.

The brand seared into the flesh of Robin's left shoulder. He screamed and fell forward. When Bill removed the brand, Rashad dumped a bucket of cold water onto the wound. They allowed Robin to rest on the ground, then Officer Burton motioned for Peter to come over.

"Take your father home. The walk'll do him good," Officer Burton said.

Peter nodded and helped his father get to his feet. The

crowd parted, dispersing at once then coagulating again on Peter's right side. Each person touched him as he passed.

At home, after putting his father to bed, Peter sat down in his mother's rocking chair by the front window, gazing out at the street. Forward, back, forward, back, rock, rock, rock.

Robin found him sitting there when he awoke a few hours later. Still in a state of minor shock, Robin stepped into the kitchen to put the kettle on. His son had not moved when he came out again. Robin looked into his face trying to discern the expression. Was it beatific, forgiving? Robin had not noticed the eyes before – cold, deep and black when they had been soft and blue yesterday.

"Tell me what happened in there," he said gently.

"I can't," said Peter, turning to look at his father.

"Can't or won't? Was it something so terrible?"

"Not at all." Peter turned again to the scene outside.

"Won't you tell me anything?" whined Robin.

"Oh, you mean anything that might ease *your* conscience?" said Peter, not looking at his father. He didn't wait for a response. "I saw Mom and Anna. Mom mentioned something about the car brakes. You fixed them yourself to save a little money, didn't you. Next time, don't forget to flush the brake lines." Peter got up from the chair and walked to his bedroom, closing the door behind him. The whistle from the kettle startled Robin. He moved quickly to remove it from the burner.

***

About a month or so later, the doorbell rang on a snowy Saturday. Peter got up from the dinner table to answer the door.

"Grandad? What are you doin' here?"

"I came to surprise you for Christmas," said the eldest Campbell, entering the house with an armful of presents.

"Great dye job on the hair. Go on out and get my suitcases will ya?"

Robin came out of the kitchen. "Dad, what are you doing here?"

"Christ, ain't anybody glad to see me?" he said as he placed the presents on the floor near the front window.

"Well, yeah, sure, Dad. I just wish you had called, is all."

Peter returned with two suitcases. "Staying for a while, Grandad?"

"I thought I might."

"Great." Peter took the suitcases into his room. "I'll sleep on the couch and you can have my bed," he said as he came back out. "Better hope Dad's on the straight and narrow. He shouldn't do anything stupid while you're here."

Charles Campbell looked from his son to his grandson. "What in hell do ya mean by that?"

**About the Author**

Carrie Connel-Gripp is a poet and fiction writer who lives in Goderich, Ontario, Canada. Her fiction has appeared in *Under the Armchair*, *Writtle Magazine* and *Bygone Days*. Her story "One-Eyed Undertaker" was published by Channillo.com in 2017. She is the author of two books of poetry, *A Day in Pieces* (2013) and *Persona Grata* (2016) both published by Harmonia Press.

# NUMBER SEVENTEEN

J.R. HEATHERTON

The smell of toast and jam and lilacs filled the dining room creating an aromatic frame around the morning's breakfast table. This was home. And there sat Father and Mother, seated opposite each other at their own respective heads of the table: Father's attention behind the pages of newsprint while Mother needled the contents of her plate, quietly worrying about what they would do to her figure. Parallel to the wall and along the table's side Jim's two younger siblings huddled together, centered like the focal point of a Rockwellian portrait. It had been his seat before they were born, and now it was their position, though Jim recalled that he tended to sit much closer to Mother, a security measure for those times when Father's scornful nature showed.

It wasn't that Father was a particularly angry or abusive man, but it was when those inevitable irrelevant statements that tend to rise in a young boy's mind were blurted out that Father showed little to no patience. By his own hand Father was more than happy to expound upon the intricacies of life without needing any provocation—subjects ranging from religion to politics, love, death, literacy, why certain races were inferior; subjects in which Father was an expert of unparalleled bona fides. Yet, here at the burgeoning age of nineteen, just shy of twenty but not far away, Jim had come to think of Father's wisdom as more of an arrogance that disguised ignorance. For Mother's sake, he tried to not argue with Father. But Jim couldn't help that he had become more vocal, more emboldened through the group and his own rebellious, youthful thoughts.

Father himself, in a way, had become more reticent when Jim was around, except when it came to his unflinching support of the State. He was a State's Patriot, an informer to the Authorities, and fiercely proud of it. Unlike all these confused sissies and whiners, whose stress of living in these times when things seemed so uncertain to them and who were easily provoked into unpatriotic thoughts, Father was made of more solid stuff; though even in his stolidity the embers of a seething fire were easily stoked given the right poker.

On such days, Mother was typically vague during Father's soliloquies, and incommunicative during Father's admonishments. When the coals of his heart burned hot she would smile and nod and mouth noncommittal words of consensus and make encouraging sounds. When the fire spread to his eyes she would refrain from any sort of interaction that might undermine his authority. It was her way. She had never disagreed with Father while Jim was growing up, a practice that continued with his two younger siblings. As Jim passed from grammar schoolboy to middle-teenaged years, and he became more and more aware of her tendency not to question or interject an alternative point of view, he wondered whether she was unwilling to do so or was incapable of questioning his facts. Was it that she agreed with him and his motives wholeheartedly like a good wife and woman should, or was it that deep down she truly wanted to disagree though to not do so was the best policy? Why would she not want to speak out, to make her voice be heard in opposition to Father's tyrannical behavior? Jim often wondered these questions, now that he was old enough to question, a full ten-years older than his twin siblings. Tyrannical—was Jim being too dramatic? Maybe she agreed with him. Or was it simply the safest alternative to favor complacency over nonconformity?

Complacency. That's precisely what it was. The whole world had fallen into complacency, in Jim's way of seeing things, that mimicked a drug-induced happiness only the most immoral of pushers wouldn't shy away from. It's why Jim had joined the group. They were the alternative that fought to expose the illness rising up from within. And the illness wasn't just the plague—

But none of that mattered right now. It was breakfast time. It was time for toast and jam and the smell of lilacs.

This was home. Nothing would change that. Jim closed his eyes and breathed in deep allowing the aromas to soak in, a little smile tugged at the corners of his mouth. He began to hum lightly. Nothing would ever change the feelings of safety found behind the walls of one's own home.

***

"Shouldn't we say something?" Mother whispered. She had leaned forward, accidentally rattling Father's cup of Earl Grey, trying to catch Father's attention from around the edge of the morning's newspaper; her eyes followed Jim as he sauntered past the table humming a light tune. Father gave his wrists a little flick, allowing the newspaper to sag into a sloppy V.

"Doesn't he know what has happened?" Mother continued, her voice low and clipped, the spoon in her hand clenched tight until her knuckles had turned ivory. "This can't be *healthy*!"

Through the clearing of black and white newsprint Father watched his eldest son. The evening before, Jim had left the house without offering any information regarding his soon to be whereabouts. But his secrecy was not the issue, for Father already knew that Jim was meeting with those friends of his again. They were the issue. That group.

*Subversives more like it,* Father thought, a pang of disgust twisting up inside of him. For months now all seventeen of them had been going on about some silly notion of a spreading plague. *What utter nonsense, a plague. Plagues were something that happened in the middle ages, and in uncivilized countries where the savages ran things. Any self-respecting citizen knows that there is no such thing as some plague being covered up by the authorities. Besides, if there were such a thing then surely the authorities would have informed the populace and would be in the process of taking appropriate actions.*

Father envisioned Jim's little group of rebels tossing

around their outlandish theories of doom and gloom. They were at it again last night. They were out causing trouble again, plotting unrest; and it was sometime during those unsupervised hours that something had gone wrong. Jim shouldn't have come home.

For some reason, he had.

*Doesn't he realize what his actions could do to this family?* The earlier disgust quickly became rising anger. *He's willingly put us at risk! What questions the authorities will have!* The stoicism in his face hardened into a mortar of contempt as he laid the paper aside and rested his arms on the tabletop. His rancor became more apparent and the family noticeably avoided eye contact with Father. It wasn't that they had anything to fear; it was just sometimes easier to avoid.

In the kitchen area, Jim had opened the refrigerator and poured himself a glass of milk before settling onto one of the barstools that rung the edge of the kitchen's countertop. He nonchalantly flipped through the pages of some old circular left lying around.

*This is incredible! He's sitting there drinking milk and reading a magazine like nothing has happened.* Father exhaled a huff. *All of these years teaching him to be proper—to be right—wasted! We're people of society, for God's sake. We're better than this. What would the neighbors think if they found out about this—this—deviant behavior?*

Around the table the family waited in Father's vague silence, which hung in the air like a guillotine's blade temporarily stayed as he evaluated the situation. He eventually drew his attention away from Jim and silently considered the two youngest children, Michelle and Joey, wondering what impact this event might have upon them. He doubted either of them truly comprehended what was going on. Even if they did, they were very young and would eventually forget given enough time. Father's thoughts turned back toward Jim. *Given enough time, all situations such as this will correct themselves. That's all that matters now, the passage of time. Soon they will be at the front door. They know where to look for the boy, where to find him. It is just a matter of playing the waiting game before they arrive and this little problem goes away.*

"Father—" began little Michelle, her soft, unsure voice broken and barely audible. But Father lifted his right hand, cut her off, indicating comments were not appreciated.

"Everyone should finish their breakfast before it gets cold," he said. It was a small cue to the family that an unspoken rule had taken effect, one that discouraged any further discussion. *And maybe the neighbors will never find out.* He winced irritably, then without further thought immersed himself back behind the erected pages of State-approved information, creating a barrier against what he no longer wanted to see, and resumed sipping his cup of Earl Grey. It was just a matter of time before the knock would come and all this went away.

Mother withdrew back into her own quiescence, carefully probing the end of a spoon into the flesh of a freshly halved grapefruit, noting to herself just how lovely the blue hues of the lilacs were set against the white and red pinstriped vase she had placed in the middle of the breakfast table: so homey. The twins stared quietly at their slices of toast and jam.

The paper's headlines were always the same; Father had read them so many times before he almost didn't need to see the print: more deaths, more terrorist activity, more operatives being rounded up. And everyday the papers reported that more and more people were buying into this self-perpetuating lie of a plague, the same one that Jim and his cronies had fallen into. Theirs was a movement that did not believe terrorists lived among the populace, that these deaths were due to some indefinable plague that was slowly spreading across the homeland like a cancer. It was a message of fear mongering, an inexplicable social disease that needed no human contact. But, every thinking person knew that it was terrorists; and to think otherwise was unpatriotic. *What was the old saying*, Father thought, *eliminate all facts and whatever remains, no matter how improbable, must be the truth.* And the truth was terrorists were here and needed to be rooted out. The State would even post snipers outside places of interest if tipped off. It had gotten to that point.

And little groups of opposition like Jim's were not helping matters.

The authorities frowned greatly on these people—these rumor spreaders, these muckrakers with their plague theory—for their interference and abject behavior. Their biased judgments were not fair. Their activities greatly hindered a fair and balanced pursuit of the truth. *Terrorists are on this soil, and terrorism is tearing this country apart in more ways than one,* Father's grip tightened on his paper. *And there are countrymen who are not loyal to the State in its time of need.* And his son was one of these people. *Something had to be done.*

Minutes continued to drift away, and still no knock came at the door. Father found his attention wandering back towards Jim sitting at the counter and nonchalantly leafing through the pages of a magazine, a nearly empty glass of milk poised at his lips. Father's anxiety for a decisive end was quickly becoming more than he could stand.

He cleared his throat and announced, "It says here there were seventeen deaths last night."

The spoon slipped from Mother's hand with a clink against the fine bone china as she stole a glance toward Jim. He still held the glass to his lips, but no longer flipped the pages.

"The authorities—"

By now, Mother had retrieved her spoon and was dribbling small words of acknowledgement between nervous spoonful's of grapefruit, "Seventeen, you say—yes—seventeen—" all the while keeping a watchful eye on Jim's reactions.

Father gave the newsprint a ruffle at the interruption

before continuing. "I was saying that the authorities—"

"Must be those terrorists again," Jim expelled after downing the last swig of milk.

Father, at this second interruption, slapped the newspaper against the table, sloshing his Earl Grey as he did so, the pages soaking up the tea and staining the print into one large splotch of runny ink. Mother continued pushing jagged bits of fruit into her mouth.

"Then again, it's always *terrorists*, isn't it," Jim said, wiggling his fingers around the word terrorists. "Everyday there's another batch of dead turning up in print and it's never an illness. Or a virus. Or a plague. No! It's always those terrorists."

Jim paused, waiting for Father to jump into the conversation, who usually leapt at an opportunity to express his views, especially if they were contrary to Jim's. Instead, Father remained silent.

"It's like that whole anthrax scare a couple years ago," Jim continued. "Remember that? The authorities were so certain it was terrorists, so they began rounding up *suspects*." Once again, he wiggled his fingers in the air at the word. "But in the end, it all turned out to be a complete hoax dreamt up by some chemical engineer who was angry over the loss of a government contract. There was never any anthrax, yet the government kept reporting all these people dying—and did so for weeks! How could they have died of anthrax if there was never any anthrax?" Jim gesticulated, throwing his hands up in the air.

He felt, more than caught sight of, Father's stare cutting into him.

"And do you know what I find to be the more interesting part," Jim continued, "if not the most disturbing? It's the fact that to this day nearly everyone still believes it wasn't a hoax. They're offended if you remind them it was reported as being so! Granted, it was only posted in the media for one day. But still, the information was out there. Can you imagine that? Even with proof that it was just some whacko bent on revenge, people still believe there's this vast syndicate of terrorists spreading anthrax around."

The table remained silent. Joey gingerly sampled his toast and jam, while Mother fussed with the grapefruit. Even little Michelle, who under normal conditions would merrily chime in with her childish logic in complete admiration of Jim, stayed mute.

Jim looked around at the faces of silence. No one returned his gaze.

"Well," he said, relinquishing his perch from the barstool and walking to the door, "this has been stimulating, but I need to get down to the library."

Father watched as Jim's hand touched the doorknob. *Just a turn of the wrist and he'll be out of this house and this will all end.*

"A few of us are getting together to—" but an apprehensive voice cut him off.

"Jim," Mother said, "do you remember last night?"

"Stay out of this, Mother. We don't need anymore questions here," chided Father.

Jim dropped his hand from the doorknob and turned with a perplexed expression. "What do you mean?"

"Well the authorities—"

"Mother," said Father, glaring at her, exigency reverberating in his voice, "we don't want this."

"What are you two going on about? What's this about the authorities?"

"Dear, we have—"

"*We* have nothing more to say in the matter," shot Father. But Mother didn't want to stop, not now after finally mustering the courage to speak. Jim needed to know. He obviously didn't remember what had happened last night. This was her son. She felt that this was her duty, as a mother, to inform him. Not the State. It showed in her eyes, silently asking for Father's consent. "Fine then," he gave in, folding his arms in resignation. "Speak to the boy if you must. But I have nothing more to say."

Mother sat down her spoon and pushed aside her plate, the remnants of the grapefruit twisted into a grotesque form that resembled a deflated ball. "Jim, dear, this is very hard for all of us to come to grips with. It's…it's so hard to understand how you, well, why you—" she glanced over to father, but he was turned away taking sips of Earl Grey.

"What's so hard to understand?" Jim pressed. "What do the authorities have to do with anything?"

Mother subconsciously fiddled with the edge of the black and white checkered tablecloth. The lilacs were indeed the perfect compliment to the table. She had done well. "Well, Jim, the authorities came here last night. They told us about—about—such shocking information about you. We've just been beside ourselves since hearing it. It's one of those visits a parent could never imagine getting in the middle of the night. But we just have to put our trust in—"

She felt the touch of Joey's fingers gently burrowing into the crook of her elbow and smiled down at him, placing a loving hand to his cheek and quivering chin, swabbing a tear from the corner of his eye with the pad of her thumb. "It's okay. There's nothing to be afraid of. They'll be here soon."

"*What* information? And they who?"

"You don't remember anything about last night?" Mother replied, her hand falling from Joey's cheek.

"No! I went out. I met with my friends. We made up some literature. I came home. The end. And now I'm here playing twenty questions."

"And that's all?"

"That's all."

"And you know nothing about the deaths last night?"

"Why would I?" exclaimed Jim in growing frustration.

"Think about it for a second, son. The authorities were very clear about this."

"My God! They don't think I know anything about

those deaths, do they?" Jim exclaimed. "They don't suspect the group, do they? I'll never give up any names. So, they better not ask for any."

Mother allowed her head to sink to her chest, no longer able to meet Jim's eyes.

"Would someone please tell me what this is all about?" Jim pleaded with the silent gathering at the table. "Won't any of you say anything? What did the authorities say?"

"That you are number seventeen." It was Father who had finally said what needed to be said, the want to put an end to all this nonsense overcoming his desire to stay the course.

"I'm what?" Jim reacted. He must have heard Father's words wrong for they didn't make sense. It was unusual for Father to speak inexplicitly.

"It's true, dear," Mother bobbed her head up and down agreeing, still looking away. "The authorities were very clear that you were number seventeen."

"Okay, so I'm number seventeen. What does that even mean?" Jim said not grasping the accusation.

"It means you're dead," Father stated flatly, as if the obvious were standing in the center of the table, kicking over the lilacs and waving a banner.

Jim was dumbfounded for an instant, trying to determine if he had heard what they were saying correctly, and then tilted his head back and roared with laughter.

"Oh my God, you all had me going! For a second, I thought you were being serious." Jim giggled with delight at the joke. "I mean, how did you all manage to pull that off with a straight face? Especially you two," he said pointing at Joey and Michelle, "sitting there all quiet and solemn. Wow!"

Father and Mother calmly watched Jim while he spoke, while he shook his laughter away. Jim came over to the empty chair at the table and flopped down into it.

"Ugh! I'm dead!" Jim exclaimed, placing his hand over his heart, rolling head back and hanging his tongue out his open mouth.

"This is not a time for levity," Father stated flatly. Jim noticed Joey and little Michelle ever so slightly scoot their chairs away from him.

"Oh, come off it. I mean a joke is a joke, but you can carry things too far you know."

"This isn't a joke," Mother said soothingly. "You died last night, dear."

"That's ridiculous," said Jim with a chuckle. "How can I be dead when I'm sitting right here in front of you?"

"That doesn't matter," said Father.

"What do you mean that doesn't matter?" replied Jim, the joke beginning to wear a little thin.

"What matters," said Mother, "is that the authorities were here and told us—"

"Told you what? That I'm dead?"

"Well, yes," Mother nodded.

"And you believed them?" Jim exclaimed.

"Yes, of course, dear," answered Mother.

"And you *still* believe them?"

Mother nodded.

"That's crazy!" said Jim incredulously. "How can you just believe something that was simply *told* to you?"

"Because the authorities said so," stated Mother. "We have proof," she said digging into a bag next to her seat and handing over an official death certification signed and notarized by the State.

"There's a problem with this, though," he said, holding the paper at length. "It's obvious that I'm not dead. I'm sitting here breathing and talking."

"But the authorities—"

"I don't care about the authorities!"

"Don't you dare speak that way in my house," Father roared, jumping to his feet, knocking over the remainder of his Earl Grey. "How dare you question the authorities in this house!"

"I'm not questioning the authorities. I'm questioning

your sanity," Jim barked back.

Joey and Michelle absently pushed their now cold slices of toast and jam around their plates, their faces pale with fear.

"Look what you are doing to your brother and sister by arguing with us," scolded Father. "Your behavior is unacceptable."

"*My* behavior? You two are telling someone who is perfectly able to sit, listen, *and* comprehend what another person is saying that he's dead."

"Because you are, son," said Mother.

"I'm not dead, for Christ's sake!"

"Oh, but you are dead," guaranteed Father, his anger in his voice now bordering closely on rage. "We have the proof."

"Because the authorities told you so? Is that it? Because you have some signed scrap of paper!"

"You cannot defy the authorities," said Father. "The fact is you died last night."

"You need to start getting used to the idea, dear," suggested Mother.

"But it's simply not true. I mean, can't you see the reality with your own eyes? Isn't my presence here in front of you proof enough?"

"My God, boy, it's time to grow up and take some responsibility for your actions," lectured Father.

"I *am* being responsible! I'm a living, thinking, breathing, and responsible person. No matter what the authorities say."

"Enough! I told you before not to question the authorities in this house, and you would do yourself well not to let it happen again."

"Do myself well? By going along and saying, 'Oh! Okay, I'm dead. Some more jam, please.'"

"Dead people don't eat jam, silly," Michelle piped up brightly.

Jim stared at her completely bewildered for a moment

before adding, "Nor do they sit around talking about it."

"Don't confuse the girl," uttered Father. "This has been hard enough for them to come to terms with." He gestured toward the two younger siblings. "Think of what you are teaching them by being so obstinate."

"Obstinate? You're telling me that I'm dead just because some petty officials told you so, and *I'm* being obstinate."

"Look. We're getting nowhere here," huffed Father, standing and slamming his palms against the surface of the table, covering them with spilt tea and jam. He stomped off to the kitchen sink, jerked on the tap and scrubbed his hands under the lukewarm water. "See if you can talk some sense into the boy," he said to Mother over his shoulder.

She gazed silently for a few moments at the flowers in the white and red-pinstriped vase. The lilacs truly were beautiful. Each flower was like a tiny cross with a watchful eye in the middle. Yes, they were the perfect compliment. She knew her duty to the family, her duty to the State. This was her moment to shine, to win one for the family and for Father. Failure was not an option; and this needed a mother's delicate touch.

"Jim, you say you're not dead," Mother began. "Fine. You can believe that if you wish."

"Mother," Jim shook his head, closing his eyes, "just look at the facts. Think about this logically."

"Son, open your eyes and look around you. Look at how we live. We have to follow the rules; it's what keeps us safe. We can't just start questioning the authorities. If we did that then how would they be *authorities*? We have to trust what they tell us. They are all that stands between truth and fiction."

Jim remained still. This couldn't be happening.

"You can go on and on about facts and logic all you want," she said, "but in the end—and you must remember this—the truth is what sets you free."

Mother watched her son's expression for a moment,

looking for clues.

"Unbelievable," Jim whispered.

"Just ask yourself, why would they lie to us?" she continued. "What would they gain from not telling the truth? Have you ever stopped to consider that? Now, son, we love you. But, fact is fact. And, more importantly, truth is truth. And the truth is that, no matter what facts you can muster up otherwise, you are dead. We know this is the truth. We have documented proof right here in our hands. The only thing preventing you from seeing this is you."

"Madness," Jim said, looking away and shaking his head at no one. "This is utter madness. You all truly believe that I'm dead."

"We know you are," said Father, still facing the sink. "You just need to know it yourself and see things our way. The right way."

The doorbell rang.

"Please, son," Mother begged. "There isn't much time. You have to realize the authorities know what's best." She paused. "You have to realize that we know what is best."

The doorbell rang again.

"Jim, in a world of lies you have to ask yourself: Who is lying to whom here?"

Jim pushed away from the table and stood up. He looked at his family, looked from face to face; half hoping still that this was all some sort of joke; looking to see if he could spot any tells like a good poker player, but instead only saw resolve in a world gone mad. Without further word, he left the breakfast table and began ascending the stairs. With each step, his mind raced with thought of escaping this nightmare. Was he even awake? Maybe this was all a dream. Maybe it was a fever. Maybe he was sick with the plague.

But he wasn't sick. And he was definitely awake. Fully awake. Maybe truly awake for the very first time in his young life. And all he wanted now was to get away, to keep his eyes open forever, to run away from this juryless death sentence.

*I'll get out of here through the upstairs window. That's it! I'll run off to a different city, maybe even a different country. I'll run off to anywhere, anywhere away from these lunatics and their State.*

Each footfall was filled with thoughts of fleeing this impending demise conjured up and conscripted by people who he had never met, who never had any personal interaction with him, and would never mourn his passing. He reached the top of the stairs. Across the landing, the door hung open to his darkened room. It seemed much darker to him now than earlier this morning, like a waiting crypt in which all he needed do was step inside to enter eternal bliss.

*I can meet up with my friends*, he thought. *Yes! That's what I'll do. The group! There's a dozen plus people I know right there. Any one of them would be willing to help....*

Then it dawned on him: Number seventeen. No. There would be no escape.

He stood framed inside the doorway. From behind he felt a slight tug at the base of his shirt.

"Jim, I picked these for you," said little Michelle as she held up a small bouquet of dianthus from Mother's garden. "Flowers are supposed to make you happy when something bad happens."

Jim took the flowers from her tiny hand and bent down to give her cheek a small kiss.

"I'll miss you," she said with a crooked smile, then turned to start padding her way back down the steps. Before her head disappeared behind the banister, she stopped and glanced back at Jim with a puzzled look. "Why did you have to die?"

"I don't know, sweetie. I guess I just had to," he said. "Sometimes the truth isn't subjective."

"That's a funny word," then she was gone.

"Yes. Yes, it is," he said to no one and entered the vault.

***

They rang the doorbell a third time, and were greeted by a stern, yet solemn, man who led them up the stairs through the smell of toast and jam and lilacs.

At the doorway of a darkened room he left them to their business.

They flicked on the light switch and stretched out a long black bag along side the length of the body lying across the bed, pushing aside a small bouquet of flowers.

They rolled the body into the bag's waiting snarl and pulled the zipper tight, placing the now full package onto a backboard so it could be carried down stairs.

They left the house at 21 Baker Street, leaving behind the aroma of home, stepping over a late edition of the morning's news waiting patiently on the front porch.

The headline read: Body of Seventeenth Terrorist Recovered.

They safely secured the body inside the back of the hearse and pulled up the street. Only then did the body let its breath out.

## About the Author

J.R. Heatherton lives in mid-Michigan where he loves to write about any subject other than himself. A middle-aged devotee of the absurd, he is currently working on a novel about a young Mexican man who comes to America to find his version of the American Dream, but instead finds porn.

# THE SHAPE OF GOVERNMENT CENTER

GENE GRANTHAM

*"No one designs architecture like that with anything good in mind."*
*–Anonymous Critic (1971)*

He coulda gone to Dartmouth.

Don't get him wrong: he liked Boston well enough. Great city, great folk (great women), great time. And while he certainly understood that Dartmouth's night life couldn't hold a candle to Boston's, at times like these he couldn't help but remind himself that he could be curled up all warm and snug in some nice quiet dorm room. See, after a certain hour the night life becomes a moot point, and you're just some cold sucker standing outside waiting for his friend to finish up his bullshit, and, on that front, he found Boston's seemingly endless skyline and labyrinthine alleys to be far less fun than sitting at home finishing off beers and watching a bad movie. So far, Saturday night was going off the rails.

"Kevin!" he hissed, not wanting to leave his spot on the bus bench. He knew the buses weren't running: those bumping, winding wanderers had gone silent hours ago, but he knew that cabbies would be prowling around, looking to snag some late night tipsy folks who had more money than common sense. Thankfully he was one such kid, flush with Christmas money from his folks, and he really didn't feel like dying of the cold or boredom while Kevin did whatever-he-was doing.

He stood up from his spot, wobbling a little from the booze swirling in his head, uncertain whether he wanted to venture towards Government Center. He had a nice seat, and the dark, quiet pit of brickwork and bunker-like pyramids wasn't something he felt like dealing with. He didn't like the train station even in the daylight hours, let alone in the inky dark of night. The handful of dim lights only helped paint the brutalist architecture as even more imposing and oppressive, to the point where the squat, cave-like entrance to the metro station underground looked less like a major transit hub and more like some best-forgotten temple to the unspeakable. Almost alien like. Or maybe it was just too much beer and not enough X-Files reruns: who was Benji to judge? "Look Kevin," he shouted, "I'm… I'm seriously not coming down there. Just get back up here, you're gonna miss the cab!"

"Come take a look at this!" Kevin finally answered back, his voice a distant and almost hushed thing. He wasn't that far: he stood in the shadows of the squat bunker at the midpoint of Government Center, but he might as well be on the moon. He was so muted both in color and sound that it was almost as though some vast crushing force held the plaza in its grip.

"I'm not," Benji warned. "I just want to go home, dude…"

"I will pay for the whole cab ride if you come help me with this," he answered back from in the darkness.

"Really?" Benji asked, skeptically. "That's like fifty bucks, man."

"And I'll totally pay it if you come give me a hand…," Kevin implored again. "You could use fifty bucks."

"I could use fifty bucks," Benji agreed, nodding. College was beyond expensive. Expensive didn't even begin to describe it: obscene would be another word. He knew from painful experience that his Christmas cash wasn't going to last half as long as he'd like.

"Fine!" Benji finally shouted, a little too loud for three in the morning. "You've bought me like the whore I am…"

"Hey man, we're all whores…" Kevin's voice answered from the shadows, always a tad too matter-of-fact-smug for Benji but, hey, fifty bucks was fifty bucks. FIFTY BUCKS.

Kevin wasn't trying to hide himself: the shadows of Government Center did that well. He was leaning up against the locked gate blocking off access to the MBTA station. During normal hours the gate was open, allowing countless throngs of college kids, shoppers, lawyers, business folks, grifters, and all-in-all, standard Bostonians to roam the plaza. Do a little shopping, maybe even see the circus if the time of year was right. At night, however, the looming surroundings cast immense shadows, so deep and absolute that they seemed almost preternaturally dark.

"What do you want, Kev?" Benji asked, growing more anxious than he felt he had right to be. It was weird: thirty feet in either direction and it was just another January night in Boston, but standing here in the dark… you could almost feel it on your skin, like insects crawling or sweat dribbling. He didn't like the way he could barely see his own hands in front of him, the way he kept thinking he couldn't feel them once they disappeared.

"So, okay, there's this thing I gotta say first…" Kevin started, and Benji wasn't sure if this was a genuine confession or just some drunk weepy thing. "See, I sorta lied about going to the party."

"What?" Benji didn't expect that. "How could you be lying? We just went to the party, dude. That doesn't make sense!"

"No, I know that, I know that!" Kevin nodded, definitely inebriated, "I mean WHY I was going. Like, I knew I was going, but not just because it was a party, you know?"

"I don't know," Benji shook his head. "I thought Kelly's birthday would be a good enough reason."

"See, it's not just Kelly's birthday," Kevin pointed out, as though Benji was supposed to have some idea of what that meant, "And I had to, y'know, get my nerves sorted out. Have a drink. So I said we were going to the party…"

"And we did…" Benji continued for him. "Man, if you were getting your nerves up to talk to Nicole you fucked that up."

"No, I… wait, do you think she'd be open to it?" He asked, distracted. "I always kinda thought she hated me?"

"Oh, she does," Benji nodded, lighting a thin Pall Mall,

"But she kinda hates everyone, so it's okay."

"That's not the point!" Kevin clarified, taking one from the pack, unified by the bond of Drunk Smokers. "The point is, I had to get my nerves up to find out if…"

"If…?" Benji repeated as Kev just sorta drifted off.

"If this was real," he suddenly said, reaching into his jacket pocket and pulling out a small object wrapped in delicate black velvet that dripped off it like liquid night. Kevin carefully unwrapped it, gingerly revealing a leather-bound journal, clasp firmly in place.

"I don't know what that's supposed to be," Benji said after a moment. "I don't know why you'd need to drink, like, a thousand Jell-O shots to get ready for it either."

"Okay, have you ever heard of Gerhard Kallmann?" Kevin started again. Sensing nothing, he added: "The famous architect. Designed this place where we're standing?"

"Is this a school thing?" Benji slowly asked. "Man, I am waaaaaaaaaaay too drunk to be doing a school thing right now."

"No!" Kev insisted. "Well, I mean, yes."

"God, no," Benji sighed. "Why are you doing this to me?"

"I mean, it just STARTED that way!" Kevin assured him. "I was doing this research on the Boston skyline, and I found out this guy, Gerhard Kallman, he was the big head behind all this brutalist architecture."

"Yeah, that's something to call it," Benji shuddered. "Feels like there's a mountain about to fall on me."

"Well, that's the funny thing," Kevin continued, "No one likes it! That's why I was digging into it. I wanted to write this whole paper on how they should, y'know, revitalize the skyline. I mean, it's the 90's for Chrissake! This city looks like Detroit in the 80's trying to look like New York in the 70's…"

"I don't know enough about architecture to know if that's true or not," Benji sighed, snubbing out his cigarette butt. "So, what are we doing? You've lost me?"

"Okay, so I went to the BPL-,"

"I told you man, you gotta explain this shit."

"The BOSTON PUBLIC LIBRARY," Kevin spelled out, a little miffed he had to, "I went there to pull up, y'know, first hand documents and shit for the paper." "God, you're such a nerd," Benji muttered, almost hissed. "Are we really here for extra credit?"

"No, man! That's what I'm trying to explain! I went to go look up the original plans, and I found this book!"

"... which you have failed to explain why it's important," Benji noted, in that snarky-sarcastic manner that drove Kev right up the goddamn wall.

"Because, this claims to be his secret journal," Kevin said smugly. "The secret life of Gerhard Kallman, in his own words!"

"I bet that's every bit as exciting as it sounds," Benji yawned, starting to feel less creeped out and more tired. "I bet a famous architect had so many skeletons in the closet. That's probably why he got into architecture, to build a closet big enough to hide all those skeletons!"

"I thought the same thing," Kev admitted. "In all the books he's just this really nice guy, nice family, great designer, all that, right? But in here..."

"Probably secretly gay," Benji guessed. "Everyone was secretly gay back then."

"What if I told you Kallmann wasn't just an award-winning genius of architecture and design?"

"I wouldn't care?"

"What if I told you Kallmann was a member of a secret society, enraptured to a Lovecraftian-esque horror from beyond imagination, integrating elaborate occult symbolism and magical principles into their work?"

"I wouldn't car- wait, what?" Benji was caught off guard by that one. He expected, at best, another gigantic discussion about how the masons were rigging the Oscars. "Are you serious?"

"That's what this book claims," Kevin said, giving the journal a jaunty little shake. "This whole Government Center thing, everyone shits on the design, but not for the reasons they should…"

"Let me see that…" Benji snatched the book from his hands, opening it up carefully. The pages were thin, vellum-like, almost translucent. The writing was faded but still quite distinct, and it was far more intricate and fancy that anything either of them could muster. There were illustrations too, strange geometric designs…

"See, I thought it was bullshit, but why would someone put so much effort into this? Like, all these charts and things, and all these pictures… this is supposed to be from the 70's, but there's designs for all the future additions they've added since then."

"But why would this secret Satanic-,"

"Not Satanic," Kevin cautioned. "Sure, there's some Golden Hermetic Order stuff, and that's, like, a little Luciferian but…"

"Okay, so this non-Satanic but still-spooky cultist architect guy, he leads this double life, right? He's publicly this great guy who's all wonderful and stuff, but he's secretly worshiping Lovehate or whatever. But then he goes and, what, accidentally returns his secret journal of wizard secrets and shit to the library?"

"Huh," Kevin stopped, musing that. "That's a good point."

"Right?" Benji answered. "Seriously man, it's probably just, like, some Dungeons and Dragons shit. Remember Steve? Steve was always too crazy about that shit, he wrote, like, essays and shit for his characters. Probably just another Steve of the world."

"Maybe," Kevin continued, with that smug tone that suggested Ben had walked straight into his trap. "But then why does the book show me finding the book in it?"

"What? That's horseshit," Benji immediately answered, instinctively, even as he felt the goosebumps on his arms.

"Show me."

"'*October 25th, 1997,*'" Kevin began to read from the book, "'*I am found.*'" Then he flipped the book around to reveal that, sure enough, there was an illustration, scratchy but very distinct, of a young man that, admittedly, looked quite like Kevin, picking the book up off a shelf.

"You didn't write that?" Benji asked, his voice a little quieter than he intended.

"Not me," Kevin asked, sobering up despite the booze. "But that's not the last entry." He picked the book back up and began to flip through it. "*November 18th, 1997, I am shown to the professionals, but they do not know what to make of me, nor do they care to discover.*"

"Who'd you show it to?" Benji asked, suddenly realizing he was taking a book at face value.

"Professor Stilton," Kevin answered, hushed. "He figured it was authentic in terms of age, but just some, y'know, stupid joke thing. Didn't bother to look at it too hard."

"Is there more?" Ben inquired, aware of how dark the mood had gotten. "There's not more, right?"

"There's one last entry," Kevin continued, and Benji just knew he was in for a whopper now from the flat tone of his voice. "Which is why I knew I had to get my nerves settled tonight, y'know? Like, when you see this you're gonna…"

"Let me see it," Benji interrupted, reaching for the book. He'd always preferred to rip the bandage off rather than slowly ease it. Just get it over with.

He wished he hadn't.

"*January 7th, 1998,*" Benji began to read from the book, almost against his will, "*The two of them will find the entrance. They will bring me home.*" He didn't need to show Kevin the picture, undoubtedly it was seared into his pal's mind just as it was eternally captured by his. The image, in faded, ancient ink, showed two very familiar looking forms lifting the gate of the station and making their way into the darkness below. At least he assumed it was a stylistic depiction of darkness, or, perhaps, thick, black coils of unknown nothingness…

"Right?" Kevin implored, finally being able to share his secret. "RIGHT?!? It's just…"

Benji wasn't sure what to make of all this. Was this some sort of stupid practical joke Kevin was pulling? This couldn't be real, right? Things like this didn't happen. It just didn't make any sense.

"It's a moot point," Benji finally figured. "I mean, we're not going to break into the station, so…"

"Well, definitely not yet," Kevin agreed. "The shadows aren't right."

"What?" Benji asked, confused. "What does that mean?"

"Well, the buildings," he pointed to the vast array of governmental structures ringing the plaza, "They cast the first layer of shadows, and the sculptures," he pointed to the similarly imposing geometric qualities of the plaza, "Those are the second layer of the three."

"And the third is…"

"This tunnel," he pointed to the locked station. "The first two layers charge the third, opening a portal."

"Gerhard didn't really hold back in his diary…"

"Problem is…" Kevin reached back into his jacket, fishing for something else, "Is that we've got some uninvited light mucking up the process."

"The streetlight?" Benji shrugged, uncertain about this. "You're telling me that the only thing stopping the Government Center station from turning into a portal to Hell-,"

"I never said Hell."

"-a portal to whatever, is that there's a streetlight?"

"Oh, no, that'd be irresponsible!" Kevin answered, as though any of this was responsible or even reasonable. "No, the portal is only active for a brief period when the stars are right, after the Winter Solstice. A period which hits its apex-,"

"Tonight," Benji interrupted with a frustrated, slightly scared, sigh. "Of course. I'm starting to see the pattern. But, again, moot point, because the streetlight is there so we-,"

Kevin pulled the pistol out of his jacket in a jerking, halting fashion, snagging it on the edge of his pocket. Benji felt his heart leap into his throat, and the world seemed to get a little quieter and fainter, like he was in a tunnel. He'd only ever seen a gun in the hands of cops. Before he could even blink Kevin pulled the trigger. What came out, however, wasn't a bang, but a stifled, hissing POP!

"Is that a fucking airsoft gun?" Benji finally stammered out. "What the fuck are you-"

After a few initial plinking shots Kevin struck home, and the streetlight cracked and fizzed, sparking one final defiant time before going dark.

"See?" Kevin said, as though he was proving some point that was apparent only to him. "Easy enough."

"Are you crazy?!?" Benji whispered as loud as he could. "They have cameras! Someone's gonna… the cops! The cops are gonna figure out-,"

"Well, we've already broken one law," Kevin figured, "Might as well help me get this gate open."

Benji stood fast as he watched his roommate squat down, grabbing the gate in both hands, and struggle to heft it up.

"Come on, I don't even think it's locked!" he implored. "We just gotta get it up high enough…"

"Bro, even if this book is real, why would I ever want anything to do with it? This is how horror movies start-,"

"Hundred bucks," Kevin grunted, still straining against the weight of the heavy iron gate. Then, sensing hesitation, he squeaked out, "Hundred bucks AND the cab fare!"

Benji really didn't like the idea of secret horrors from the occult world of architecture… but, on the other hand, that was a lot of money. Besides, he was a young college kid; whoever heard of one of them getting into too much trouble? More like than not this was all some stupid prank of Kevin's anyway, but Benji was gonna hold him to that money.

"Fine," Benji said, displeased and disquieted by his choice, but convinced by the shine of the lucre. "I'll do it." He leaned down and helped lift the gate up. Between the two of them it was still quite the project, but they managed to get it high enough for them to squeak through before letting it slam back down with a thunderous boom.

"You won't regret it," Kevin assured him, panting, exhausted from the effort. "Gonna be a great time!"

"I get paid even if you're wrong, right?" Benji coughed and panted out, wanting to stake his claim first and foremost.

"Sure, sure…," Kevin said, smugly, positive he was right. "Money's gonna be all yours."

They stood up, dusting themselves off, peering into the darkness below. The station sloped downward swiftly, and the escalator, normally rumbling constantly, was now eerie and still. There was little lighting, only the flicker of dim emergency bulbs, ancient sodium things behind yellowed plastic flaked with long-dead moths.

As they started to take a few cautious steps into the station Benji noticed a sound. It was faint, and, at first, he just figured it was a train, but he quickly realized it was different from the standard noises they made. Trains might thrum while on standby, they might groan with their environmental systems, hiss as the compressors empty and fill, but they didn't do what this sound did.

"Do you hear that?" Benji asked as they continued down the stairs. "Like this weird…."

"Pulse," Kevin answered. "I feel it in my chest, like a bass drum."

"Probably just a train doing… train stuff," Benji lied, eager to whistle in the dark.

They made their way down to the flat expanse of the

loading platform, now dim and absent of commuters. The darkness down here was beyond extreme: it was like coal, or like stepping into outer space. There was no light here, nothing to differentiate the next step from deep down the train tunnels.

"Where are we even going?" Benji whispered before they went and further. "Are we just gonna bump around in the dark or…?"

Kevin didn't answer though. In the darkness Benji couldn't even tell what direction Kevin was looking in, but he could sense that he was captivated by something. He started to jab at his friend, to ask what it was, when he realized that, out of the corner of his eye, he could see movement, just barely highlighted by the distant dim glow of some light or another. He stopped, frozen, assuming it was a security guard, and that they were simply seconds away from getting busted and having to call their parents and explain why they needed bail money bad.

Why couldn't it have been a guard?

It wasn't though. It was nothing. Nothing but darkness. Yet that very darkness seemed to swirl around itself, to pull in, constrict, and then relax. Somehow the night itself was flexing, shifting, almost like smoke billowing in the station, or being trapped in the veins of some great monstrous being. An absence of light itself, roiling like an unkempt pot, "breathing" with the same staggered pace of the strange sound reverberating in the air.

"What… what…" Benji tried to ask, but he didn't raise his voice above those first few breaths. He realized he could feel it shifting around him, moving like vast, translucent tentacles, like a firm breeze, wrapping around his body, pulsing and breathing around him. He could feel it move upon his skin, through his air: with a sickening knot in his guts he realized he could feel it INSIDE HIM, within his lungs, his stomach, his very heart… soon his entire being was thrumming along, matching the beat of whatever vast engine seemed to be at work.

He didn't make a conscious decision to run. It was simply panic, an instinctive, animal voice within him that finally spoke up and told him he needed to move immediately. Unfortunately for him the great invisible lungs he found himself trapped in had a different idea, and quickly he found a vast pressure pulling at him, trying to push him down, backwards, anywhere but forward. Soon it became an unbelievable, almost electric feeling, and he knew something immense and nonsensically immaterial was upon his back, something he had absolutely no desire to turn and face. Instead he gave into that monkey-brained instinct and took off towards the… tunnels, perhaps? He didn't know, nor care; his mind shrieked one command over and over: RETREAT… RETREAT… RETREAT… REATREAT.

"Come back!" Kevin shouted, but his voice was muffled, strange, distorted, like coming through an aquarium. Benji kept running, ignoring it, tumbling, continuing on all fours, scrambling over any obstacles that came his way. Most he recognized as mundane aspects of the train station: a bench, a trash can, a vending machine, but quickly he started to feel things he didn't recognize. A strange cylinder of warm, almost marble material, which buzzed like a wasp's nest when he got near it. A gelatinous mass with sharp, cold things coming out of it, like the decorative swirls upon a fence. Something that cried out like a baby but felt like a sea cucumber.

He didn't dare to imagine what they might be. Not even for a hundred bucks.

When he saw the light he assumed, at first, that it had to be a good thing. Trapped in a living pit of swirling darkness, light would be the most obvious escape. Maybe it was the exit, or maybe it was a person with a light, who knew? He didn't care, he just ran towards it as fast as he could, his lungs sucking down the darkness in gulping mouthfuls, no choice left now but to push through it and keep running.

"Help me!" He screamed, not quite sure what he needed help from exactly, but knowing on an animalistic level that he was most certainly imperiled. "Please, help!"

The pulsing noise was loud now, so loud it seemed to cause the very mortar of the station to grind against itself. He stumbled, landing on something hard and metallic that slammed him like the dickens. He realized it was a rail, a train rail, and moreover, he could feel the pulse vibrating within, spreading, amplifying, the whole WORLD beginning to vibrate sympathetically. He could even feel the darkness running between his fingers, crawling on the metal like eels in a stream.

The light began to grow, engorging itself from a pinprick into a vast plume, and he began to realize it was far too high up to be another person from his perspective. Suddenly he put two and two together and realized if he was sitting on a train track watching a light coming towards him… He scrambled for safety, feeling his way out of the train pit, rolling onto the platform. The light was growing closer and closer, but as it moved the darkness barely budged from its path, like the thickest fog he'd ever seen.

As loud as the pulse of the station was, he became aware of another sound. A shuffling, breathing sound, thick and wet, and a rhythmic popping like immense knuckles shuffling. He was frozen as he realized it was coming from the light and that it was ALIVE, its shuddering, flexing form vague but certainly a living being. He had few options, so he went with the one that hit him first: he opted to just lay there on the ground and feign death, hoping either to be ignored or, god willing, killed quickly.

The thing with the light was no train, though it rode the rails and was the same size. For starters, it was translucent, an immense log-like being made of shivering jelly with the faintest tinge of silver. Within it were strange organs, chiefly one that glowed at the front like an immense lantern. Within it great veins pumped, and upon its skin, flaps like immense ventilators farted out plumes of steam, drawing in ragged, phlegmy breaths. It rode upon great shifting bones suspended with a membrane, walking upon its own knobby haunches like some sort of horrible caterpillar.

It paid no attention to Benji, continuing its slow, messy journey. As it traveled its nubs popped and cracked, shifting with the gooey sack that it rode upon. It was huge and long, far, far longer than any train he had seen, and he watched as it passed him by. Suspended with its gelatinous snake-like body were other organs and veins, glowing in their own indistinct way, but there was more than that. There were passengers in there; great tubular bodies with bunches of eyes at the tops and great wings floated, frozen as they were transported from some strange nothing to some other perplexing someplace.

Eventually the fleshy caravan passed him by, leaving him swamped in the thick mucus it exuded. He wanted to wretch and panic as the goo overtook him, but he waited, bubbling away, until he was positive the thing was gone. He erupted forth, gasping for air, wanting to be sick, but the pure fury of adrenaline keeping him firmly in control. He could feel the darkness in the air shifting, following the thing down the tracks, and he knew this was his chance. He took off, using his mental map to imagine where the stairs must be from here. He'd come through this station plenty of times, he could do it once more if he just concentrated.

He nearly broke his neck crashing into the locked turnstiles, tumbling to his feet, gasping for air, but he was so grateful to be near the exit his heart practically leapt out of his chest. He climbed on all fours up the stairs, seeing the first glimpse of light above. As black gave way to gray he almost wept for joy as he finally saw his own hands, slime covered and bruised, before him. He climbed the stairs, crashing into the grate at the top, having entirely forgotten about it.

"Fuck it," he muttered, grabbing it in both hands and heaving as hard as he could. It took two to open the gate, or one person who was abso-fucking-lutely determined to escape. Just as he thought his muscles might shred like newspapers he managed to wedge himself beneath, throwing himself free before it came slamming down behind him.

He lay there on the cobble stones of Government Center, eyes firmly closed, gasping for air, not sure what to do next. He realized with a sinking feeling that Kevin was still in there. Sure, this was technically the guy's fault, but how was he supposed to know what was going to go down? Besides, he met Kevin's parents on Family Day, and he'd feel terrible to have to tell them their son was eaten by… who knows what? He didn't even have the words to describe what he'd seen down there.

As he opened his eyes he realized he didn't have words to describe a lot of things now.

This was not the sky he'd left behind.

Above, in a deep, dark sea tinged of rose, sat three great moons, one a lush green. The stars were flickering things of green and black, but even they were but a dim backdrop for the immense creatures that swam in the skies above him.

Benji was able to wrench his eyes from the horrors above long enough to realize that this skyline was nothing like that which he had left behind. The brutalist architecture was still there, but now it was covered in great blood-red lines and runes, languages that he could not possibly know the meaning of, but yet their messages of terror and conquest were clear. Instead of skyscrapers there were vast monstrosities, lumbering slug-like things, or snail-creatures the size of towers. Where the Prudential Center once loomed, there was a massive stalk, twitching and grasping to feed on anything that flew too close to its seven mouths.

"Well, that was something," Kevin said from behind him. Benji twirled around, desperate for something to anchor onto in this unknown realm, something, anything from the normal world. He was terrified he was alone here, the only human in a world of nightmares.

What stood behind him was not even vaguely human. It was shaped like a tree, only made of thin, wisp-like strands, white-as-bone, and as it spoke to him it shimmered chromatically. From its great trunk crawled a thousand legs, so fine and thin as to be almost imperceptible. It loomed over Benji, its immense "foliage" made of grasping claws and finger-like appendances, all eager to grapple at it.

"Seriously though," the thing sighed through its dozen mouths in a voice that sounded like a drowning harmonica, "Guess I owe you a couple of bucks. What do you say we go find an ATM?"

Somewhere overhead a thing like a combination of a discus and a bat laughed and laughed and laughed as it watched the human run off into the city of Bones and Nightmares…

## About the Author

Gene Grantham (19??-) hails from Maine. He enjoys spinning yarns that combine the easy-going storytelling traditions of his homeland with sinister occult undertones and a liberal dose of dark comedy. His first novel THE RETURN OF MAJORANE JANE has been heralded by readers as "a story" and "readable".

You can follow and find more of Gene's work here: www.patreon.com/genegrantham.

# THE ALMOST CANNIBAL

MORGAN K. TANNER

You know, cannibals have quite the reputation. I'm not saying that this is unjustly bestowed upon them but let's be honest, if you hear the word *cannibal* you either think of a tribe of primitive, almost-cavemen beasts in an unknown corner of the Amazon, or some psychopathic crazy. And yes, you'd probably be right to think that. Many of our judgements of people who are different from ourselves are ingrained into our minds from an early age. That ridiculous word, *morality*, has a lot to answer for.

Aren't these 'cannibals' just hungry? Granted they crave the taste of meat that was once alive and *thinking*, but just because they don't love, say, avocados does that make them sick in the head?

Still not convinced?

I think I may need to quickly clarify that I am *not* a cannibal, certainly not in the sense that you're thinking of. I don't enjoy feasting on the dead flesh of men, women, or children. I'm no killer or deranged sociopath, and the act of taking another human life frankly turns my stomach.

No, I prefer my dinner to be alive.

I have explained myself to Rachel over and over, but she still seems to think I'm insane. Although I doubt she really understands me. She clanks her chains, writhes on the soiled mattress, and screams at me to let her go without really listening to what I'm telling her.

"Please let me go, I won't tell anyone," she moans, *constantly*. I really thought that this was some Hollywood cliché, invented by lazy script writers to invoke some kind of humanity in their audience, but it appears that this statement is pretty accurate. I wonder now how many of them were writing from personal experiences. It would explain a lot.

Rachel is unconscious at the moment. I gassed the room earlier so she'll be out for another hour or so. But that gives me all the time I need. I'm not that hungry right now anyway. I don't have the need or ability to exert much energy in my condition, so my stomach has shriveled from the size it once was.

But it's the taste. Oh, the taste. Ethereal, clandestine, magical; better than anything you could imagine passing your lips and coalescing with your taste buds. That divine moment when I feel it melting in my mouth, it's comforting and exhilarating warmth passing through my trembling body. That is what I crave.

I'm a junkie, a slave to the flavor.

I suppose now I should introduce you to my humble assistant. I don't like to refer to him as a servant, that makes me sound very pompous and self-important, when I'm anything but. Even though he *serves* me per se, I like to think he is merely assisting me on my magical journey of culinary discovery.

He doesn't have a name, I've never really thought to give him one. It has never been necessary. There's only him and me in the basement so it doesn't really get too confusing. But when speaking of him to one of the dishes (by dishes I mean the likes of Rachel) and to you, I just refer to him as He.

He is a scrawny, hunch-backed rodent of a man. His bones protrude from his paper-like skin as though they are about to explode from his body like shopping in an over-stuffed plastic bag. His wrinkled face is gaunt and droops like molten wax, probably brought about by the years of looking up at me from his cowering posture.

He is not the kind of creature you could look favorably upon, a face not even a mother could love. But he is the very being responsible for where I am today. And for that I cannot thank him enough.

I can't remember where He came from exactly. Perhaps he was a gift from some higher being, I sure as hell deserve one after everything I've been through. But it feels like He has always been here with me, tending to my every need, nourishing me both physically and emotionally. He has changed my life.

He slumps over to me with a plate of food that rattles

in his quivering hands. It's not gourmet dining by any means, but it's exactly what I want right now. He knows me so well. It's part of the scab from Rachel's elbow. It's been crusting up for the past week, slowly turning from red to brown. I have been salivating every time I look at it.

Along with the scab is a small portion of fingernails. He hasn't dressed the plate, the nails don't encircle the scab like they would do on a Michelin-star restaurant's. But that doesn't bother me in the slightest.

Her toenails, I'm saving. I've had my eye on them for a while; those thick, crumbly, fungus-infested chunks of Heaven. Every day they grow and every day their flavor is maturing like a fine cheese.

The scab is simply wonderful. I savor it like it's my last meal on earth. I munch greedily on the nails but keep one in my mouth, placing it behind my top lip where it will moisten and entertain me for a good few hours.

"Thank you," I say to He, "make sure her bandage is clean would you?" He sniffs and gurgles something before clambering over to the sleeping buffet, inspecting her back.

*Mmmm*, her back. Last week, while she was unconscious, Rachel's skin was sliced carefully by He, leaving a large flap of flesh the size of my hand. This flap was folded back while the resulting wound was cleaned and covered with a sterile gauze bandage. The pink tissue is healing well and the flap is drying out nicely, He tells me. At least I *think* that's what He was saying. In a couple of days it will be perfect, like a piece of beef jerky, but crunchier. I'm looking forward to that more than I can tell you.

For a strange, Golem-like creature, He is astonishingly good at what he does for me. Most people, I imagine, would struggle to perform these minor surgeries he carries out on an almost daily basis. He has talent, I cannot deny it. An almost Saint-like talent.

"Get the cheese grater on her arm for me," I tell He. It

has been soaking in soapy water for a few hours to rid it of the previous blood stains, these will ruin the flavor. I relax in my chair and watch He scamper to the bowl where he removes the grater and dries it on one of the fresh towels I have provided.

He takes the grater and, using the side with the tiny holes used for grating Italian hard cheeses, begins gently rubbing Rachel's forearm. He snarls as he works and the metal rattles against her manacles, but he is doing a fine job. A damn fine job. He has such a delicate touch.

A graze quickly develops and in seconds her arm darkens as a delightful plasma jus flows from her flesh. She murmurs something, groggy from the effects of the gas, then her eyes suddenly open. She cries, as though she doesn't know where she is. He jumps back, dropping the grater with a large clang which reverberates around the basement.

Then her pain really hits home.

"What are you doing, you freak?" she screams at He. Her hand reaches for her bloody arm and her bravado disappears instantly. It's replaced by pathetic sobbing. He knows what to do. He quickly wipes her blood with a tissue and is away before Rachel can even attempt to lash out at him.

He hands me the crimson tissue. "Thank you," I say. The blood lines my throat like a savory cough sweet as I suck on it like a kid with an ice cream. I settle back and watch her pain and desperation intensify while I enjoy my palate cleanser.

You are probably coming to regard me as some sort of monster, as I relax with my tissue of blood whilst watching an innocent suffer. But it's not like I'm going to kill her. OK, she *might* die, but it won't be me that kills her. It will probably be the injuries, however superficial they may be, that will be her doom. But I didn't inflict them. *He* did.

And what is so despicable about that, really? Do you feel pity for the chef that burns his hand on the oven door, or slices off the tip of his finger while he's preparing your meal in that fancy restaurant? Do you tell the waiter 'no don't worry, that's fine, I don't mind waiting another half an hour for my meal'? No, you don't. You're paying good money and if you don't receive the service to the expected standard then you are entitled to be displeased.

Rachel suffers like the chef. In fact, she cries herself to sleep every night. OK, I may help her drift off with the gas that I have pumped into her room every so often, but it's what she wants. Although she never tells me this.

"I am leaving you for a while, my love. Some of us have work to go to," I say. "Please don't rub that arm too much, we want it to scab over nice and quickly don't we?" I lick my lips and throw the less-bloody tissue to the floor. He will clean it up for me.

Rachel mouths something at me but it's inaudible. Her eyes are so full of shimmering tears that I find it impossible to tell what she is thinking. But I think she's saying 'thank you.'

Before leaving her I pause and stare at the thick layers of calluses adorning the soles of her pretty feet. I look forward to He shaving them off for me. Like chewy potato skins. Delicious.

I enter the elevator, which is incongruent to the rest of the place. It's shiny buttons and sleek, metal doors highlighting how dark and dingy it actually is down here. As the door closes I hear yet more cries and whimpers from the basement.

What, did you think Rachel was the only one down here? Seriously? Oh come on, there's barely enough sustenance there for a small child.

He is busy preparing my evening meal. Jason, the young man I keep chained to the boiler, produces such a vast array of foot fungus from the high temperature he's exposed to there. And then there's his tangy sweat. By God it's good.

Judging by the noise Jason is making I'm sure He is

getting to work peeling the sores from between his toes. And I know that he has a vast collection of verrucae under there, too, complete with crusty skin. I hope that He decides to remove a couple for later. He's been known to treat me from time to time.

And wasn't that Annie screaming just then? Her acne juices up nicely, like miniature mountains of shiny, greasy mustard on her pained face. They go so well with the various pieces of skin which He strips from her, like chips and a dip.

The fingernail in my mouth can also double as a toothpick. Very useful when those rogue strings of flesh get caught in there. If I have enough time I usually floss my teeth with a piece of hair, although their locks do become rather weak and greasy after a couple of weeks down here. I suppose I could get He to wash them occasionally. But would that impair the flavor? I'm not entirely sure. Best have a think about that.

The elevator is almost silent as I ascend to ground level, dreaming of my meal to come. A selection of tapas to be washed down with the finest tears of my subjects. The secret ingredient is fear. He shall do me proud, he always does.

A *ping* announces I have reached my destination. The door slides open.

"Are you ready to go?" I'm surprised to see my driver, Michael standing there, dapper as always in his black suit. He could be a hearse driver by the look of him. Come to think of it, he's not a million miles away from that vocation. "The car's outside. I think you're going to be great today," he adds with an enthusiastic grin.

As we head outside into the blazing sunshine Michael puts a hand on my shoulder and gives me a motivational squeeze. "How are the mushrooms getting along down there, boss?"

"They're doing just great, Mike. Just great." Yes, Michael believes that this is what I spend so much time doing down there. And why would he think any different? I don't look like the kind of man who does what I do.

It's a short drive to the church and the road outside the sleek building is already littered with cars as people try to politely bustle their way inside. Although for most, it's a struggle. Walking sticks, wheelchairs, walking frames, elderly folks guided by relatives. Then there's the ones with the invisible ailments. None of them want to miss the main event. And neither do I.

There's to be a motivational speaker addressing them shortly. Kind of like an inspirational life coach, but I don't favor that particular term. It seems as though word has got around. I'm quite the mini-celebrity.

Yes, friends, it is I who will be speaking to these luckless fools. For all the tribulations life throws indiscriminately into their paths, the only thing they need is for a stranger on a stage with a microphone to tell them it is all part of God's will, The Master Plan. And if they are willing to pay me and revere me for telling them that everything will be OK in the end, who am I to crush their dreams?

Michael helps me from the car and escorts me to the rear entrance. I bid him farewell as he leaves me to go and park the car. I'll meet him later, maybe I'll have a new friend with me.

The Minister welcomes me with a firm handshake and a kiss on each cheek then takes me inside. I feel like some kind of rock star backstage, such is the buzz around me. People are patting me on the back and shaking my hand, and I have a lot of 'God bless you's' thrown at me.

Indeed. Bless me.

I'm shown to the stage and positioned while the murmur of anticipation from the other side of the curtain crescendos. I can not just hear it, I can *feel* the excitement building. I think of Rachel's hard-skinned feet then take in a deep breath. I rub my tongue over the fingernail that's still in my mouth and picture myself gorging on her calluses until I'm close to vomiting.

"Just another minute," the Minister tells me, breaking the reverie. I wave in acknowledgement, clearing my head of the fantasies that will soon become flesh. No pun intended.

A few minutes later the audience goes silent from beyond the curtain. They've probably killed the lights.

*Here we go.*

The curtain raises and a spotlight hits me in the face. The crowd roar. I raise the mic from my lap. I can't see anything bar the blinding light but I picture chewing on a rind of dried heel skin or a piece of crusty snot, and smile.

"Wow, thank you so much." I never fail to marvel at how strange it is to hear my own voice amplified around me. But they can't hear me, not yet. Their applause is deafening and enthusiastic. But at least my eyes are adjusting to the light. Yes, I can see them now. I hold my hand up and try again.

"What a kind welcome, thank you. God bless you all." They go even crazier at this. It's like it's some kind of magic word.

Eventually the crowd settles somewhat, apart from a couple of guys who writhe on the floor like they're being electrocuted in front of me. They're really getting into this.

"As I look out on so many of you gathered here today, I am saddened by the travesties that have been grievously bestowed upon you." I eye the rows of wheelchairs whose occupants stare at me with a desperate hope in their tear-filled eyes. "What have we done to deserve this?" I shrug my shoulders, my gaze darting among them. "Surely there cannot be a God who would inflict such horrific circumstances on his adoring children. What sort of God would do such a wicked thing? This is something I have pondered for many years. Since my accident I have come to appreciate Him in a whole new, and wonderful light. And you can, too."

I pause, knowing from previous experience that this is

the moment the first round of applause starts. It's a knowing, confident applause. One that says 'yes, this is what I came to hear, but let's not get too carried away just yet, let's see what else he has to say.'

"I could have easily slammed the name of The Lord," I continue, "moaned to the world that I didn't deserve such cruelty. 'Poor me, poor me,' I could say, reaching out for sympathy from anyone who would listen. But where would that really get me? Would I be any happier? I'd still be in this wheelchair, I'd still be unable to run in a sunlit field, or swim in the bright blue ocean. I would still be sentenced to a life like this. But I'd also have bitterness controlling me, determining every moment of my existence. And what good does that do for anyone?"

Applause. Genuine, heartfelt applause.

"In times of adversity it is important to step back from your emotions and look at life as a tapestry sewn from dreams, experiences, and hopes." The room is now silent again. All eyes are upon me as I wheel myself across the stage like a vehicular Messiah.

"And who is responsible for this tapestry? Is it the individual? Well, yes, to some extent. But who supplies the needles, the cotton, the *skills* to produce such a work? That needs to come from somewhere else. Or some*one* else."

There is a smattering of claps, although most of them don't understand what I'm telling them. I glance at the Minister who sits with a straight back and a beaming smile. He nods encouragingly at me.

"You," I address the crowd, "if you were to begin work on your own tapestry right now, what would it depict? A morbid, blackened, diabolic shambles of a scene enraged by your negativity and anger? You call it your life, your existence. But with a little help, with the correct tools to aid you, you can transform your desolate artwork into a thing of beauty that not only becomes loved by you, but is enjoyed and treasured by those around you for many years to come."

I clear my throat during another ripple of applause. A man with only one leg is nodding vigorously. I eye his stump, wondering what culinary delights I could extract from the scar tissue left there. The dry, flaky skin would be like parmesan cheese and bring any dish to life.

"*He* inspires *my* tapestry. *He* provides me with everything I need. *He* motivates me to complete my work so that it will indeed inspire others. Without him I don't think I could go on. We all need someone like this. Someone to help us, to *invigorate* us. Someone to give our lives meaning.

"Despite everything that has been thrust into my life, against my will, I say this, and believe me when I speak."

Dramatic pause. They're loving this.

"With every ounce of truth I possess, I am happy. My life is filled with happiness. When I fight against my physical hurdles from getting out of bed, to washing, to feeding, He shows me the way. Without the constant attention that He provides I would be nothing. He gives me love I would never have thought possible to know. He attends to my every waking need. He is there for me, and He is there for *you*."

This is all they need. The floor erupts as they stand, en masse, and flood me with rapturous applause. Yet more of them fall to the ground, their bodies twitching and their mouths spewing forth utter nonsense.

I wheel myself across the stage where people hobbling with walking sticks and frames attempt to get close to me, to touch me, in the hope that my positivity can somehow infiltrate their pathetic and worthless lives.

If only they knew who *He* really is. How He is merely a servant to fulfill my own deranged happiness on this wretched earth.

"Thank you, God bless you all," I scream, but it's drowned out by the pandemonium before me. I have more to say, and during the majority of these speeches I manage to go on with yet more theological absurdity.

But not today. It seems as though my work here is done.

Although not quite. I came here for more than adoration.

I spot a young lady staring at me from a few rows back. She's standing and applauding like the rest of them. But there's something about her. My eyes are drawn to her. My pulse quickens and I almost feel a twitch in my foot, something I seldom experience since the car accident.

She is a big girl, not just fat but tall, too. My mind races and I can almost taste the sweat from between her folds. I try to avoid licking my lips but I must fail as she's now smiling. I hold up a finger and nod to backstage. She nods, too, with understanding. I will meet this groupie later. I will invite her back home with me and she will accept my proposal. I find it outrageous how these God-fearing folk are always so easy to jump into bed with someone who they believe holds the answers they have been looking for.

Spreading their legs in the name of God. Pathetic. You may argue that she deserves what's coming to her, but I hate to be so judgmental.

Michael knows not to ask questions, he's been my driver long enough now. He'll smile, give an approving wink, and wish me all the best. God knows, he's done it plenty of times before.

Maybe this girl will have a friend? That would be the perfect end to this magical day. There's plenty of room in the basement.

And I'm always hungry.

**About the Author**

Morgan K Tanner is a writer, drummer, and golfist currently residing in the English countryside. The quiet surroundings make it an ideal place to write, drum, and hide the bodies. The sound of the typewriter is perfect to drown out the hum of the torture equipment. His works of fiction and threats have appeared in the mailboxes of many a celebrity, who then sells their story to the tabloids, claiming that they are being 'terrorized.'

You can praise or abuse him by visiting
morganktanner.com or find him on Twitter
@morgantanner666.

# BLACK LUNG HAY FEVER

S.E. CASEY

Visible waves of heat rose from the sea of wheat. Buoyed by the updrafts, motes of chaff the size and shape of locusts hung in the air. The yellow field wasn't much to look at, not a tree, rock cropping, or silo to provide any point of reference in the hill-less landscape. Yet, the old-timers sitting outside Jasper's Corner Store stared into it day after day as if vigilant for some sinister arrival.

The lone landmark of the flat field was a useless totem, only visible at sunset and easily dismissed. The silhouetted figure would only appear against the backdrop of the crimson pre-night sky. Stuck in the same pose, the scarecrow's arms were raised toward the heavens as if exalting the coming of the night. Set up on a riser, its legs were similarly splayed, assuming a wide base as if trying to stand without aid of its pole.

The sunset's straw specter had been marooned out in the field the same way for so long, it barely registered with Randall's residents. The durum wheat had soured long ago, useless even as livestock fodder. Indeed, the scarecrow not serving the town any practical purpose, they didn't even have a name for it. Even the old men, the only people in town who would have witnessed any activity in the fields, never called it by name. Sipping their beers, they would sometimes trade short quips of childhood memories of the former industry, but if they remembered what it was, they never spoke it.

The backlight of the setting sun obscured any of the scarecrow's features. It was just a smudge against the horizon, its details hidden from the town. If its eye buttons had fallen off, or its denim overalls had been eaten away by weevils, or its straw hair had blown out from under its floppy palm hat, no one would know. If its burlap mouth was torn into a smile or a frown, no one remembered.

Strangely, it was only in the short interval between day and night that its outline was visible. During the day, the distortions of the blaring sun bent the white light around the straw figure, hiding it in plain sight. Despite being lashed to a post, under the sun it disappeared with the deftness of a master illusionist.

It was the hottest day of the summer. In the Midwest drought season, it hadn't rained in weeks despite the humidity. The sun seemed late to set as if it took on a sadistic personality and wanted to beat down the land for some extra time. Against the delayed crimson sky, two shadows stood in the middle of the field. Many distrusted their eyes, believing it to be some optical illusion, a product of the heatwave. However, as the background color deepened, there could be no doubt. Squatting beside the field's scarecrow was a smaller one, it too, arms raised and legs splayed like da Vinci's Vitruvian Man.

The town reacted dully to the news unwilling to be jolted out of their afternoon routines. Camped out under the share of the corner store, the old-timers sipped their beers. Under the wide brims of their weathered cowboy hats, their stares were pinned to the new addition on the horizon. However, they seemed neither surprised nor worried.

How anything new could be built so far out in the disused field was a mystery. The ground was too rutted and overgrown for even the most rugged trucks or jeeps. The large threshers with the crawler treads was the only way it could be traversed. But with no need for these vehicles since the crop went bad, long ago had they been sold off to farmers in faraway places, scrapped for parts, or simply left to rust out in abandoned barns.

A few of the townsfolk asked the old-timers if they had seen anyone entering the fields.

The old men shook their heads. They hadn't.

The twin dark profiles of the two scarecrows returned the next day and the day after that. Whispered rumors spread around Randall.

It came to a head at noon on the third day, an angry woman barreling onto Jasper's porch.

"Hey!"

Vivian Traylor didn't need to get the attention of the men. In her fury, she could hardly be missed.

"You know what's out there don't you? Have you seen Violet? Did she go into the fields? Was she taken?"

Vivian's daughter had been missing for three days.

However, if her accusation surprised them, the old-timers didn't flinch. They shook their heads. They hadn't seen anything.

Vivian stood her ground. She was a rare single mother in the god-fearing community. She hadn't been raised in Randall nor did she have any relatives in town to vouch for her. As an outsider, she bore her loss alone, perceiving a lack of sincerity in any of Randall's rescue efforts.

The town froze for a long minute. Vivian continued to fume. The old timers continued to sit, but didn't drink their beers. Those shopping at Jaspers stayed inside. No one dared to step out onto that shivering porch.

Vivian finally bent down to look into the old men's eyes tucked under their cowboy hats. Her body language softened. They were telling the truth. Wiping away her tears, she allowed them a reluctant nod. Shooting a disgusted glance to the many who watched her from the windows of Jasper's, grocery bags in their hands, she limped off the porch toward the field.

The scarecrows were hidden in the glare of the midday sun. Still, Vivian strained for a glimpse among the waving stems and spikes. It was impossible to pinpoint exactly where to look despite seeing them every sundown. It was as if the mind held two distinct memories of the field—one in the day, the other at sunset—and was incapable of overlaying the two. The ocean of wheat remained inscrutable, only the contrast of the red end-of-day sky would reveal their location.

She would wait.

*Do you care for a seat ma'am?*

Vivian spun around to face the old-timers, but she failed to place the gravelly voice with a face. Vivian studied the old men, all Randall natives who despite the town's demise had never left. There was an empty seat courtesy of Bob Brannum's passing. Pancreatic cancer had taken him during the winter and his chair hadn't been sat in since.

Deciding the offer sincere, she declined with an appreciative nod and turned back to the sun-drenched fields.

Under the shade of Jasper's awning, the men shrugged and sipped their beers.

The spectacle soon drew a crowd. The town was too small for this drama to go unnoticed.

When the outline of the scarecrows materialized against the first embers of the setting sun, Vivian stepped into the field. Ghost-like clouds of pollen haunted in her wake as she angrily batted away the willowy stalks to clear a path. Vivian stumbled badly, the ground uneven and rutty, untilled as it had been for decades. She also battled over the hardened clumps of dead plant matter, twisted gnarls where the crop had died, rotted, and congealed. Only with her maternal resolve did she manage to fight through.

The leering townspeople watched as she disappeared into the jaundiced wheat. Couples held hands, men clenched their fists, and women nervously twisted their rings. They charted Vivian's progress by the shaking tops of the wheat surface. Soon, however, they lost her trail in the failing light. Even Vivian's sobbing cries for Violet vanished too, washed out by the call of the nighttime crickets. With nothing else to see, the town would have to wait until morning to know what she would find.

The crowd dispersed excepting the old-timers. For hours yet, they sat and drank their seemingly endless beers.

***

A rapt audience greeted the sunset. The entire town found an excuse to be idling outside Jasper's Corner Store. Nothing had changed. Vivian hadn't returned. Violet was still missing. The old-timers sat as usual, every seat taken except for the one.

In the first blush of sunset, silhouettes of three scarecrows surfaced. Many eyes were cast to the old-timers.

The old men shrugged and sipped their beers.

The blank profiles deep in the field were dreadfully motionless, the summer's thick humidity holding them corpse-still, not allowing even a flutter of clothing or loose straw. Nonetheless, the town watched the contorted shadows until they disappeared under the pall of a moonless night.

Imaginations stirred. Fantasies inflamed. Anything could be out there in the impenetrable darkness: a grand feast underway, a celebration of lovers, the building of a steeply gabled mansion, a sharpening of knives, a worship of some deranged deity... But no one would ever know. The only thing visible in the sinister theatre was the dull light of the stars hovering above in their meaningless patterns.

Despite the velvet curtain of night being drawn shut, no one went home. There would be no sleep in Randall given the insinuation of this nocturnal menace.

A pick-up truck screeched to a halt off the side of the road. The men that had snuck away from the spectacle exited the truck and grabbed the gas cans that filled its bed. They doused the first row of the wheat field. Retreating a safe distance, the fire chief lit the starter points. Aided by the accelerants, the dry stalks caught quickly. The easterly wind that always seemed to strengthen after twilight propelled the blaze outwards into the heart of the field, the dry husks generously sharing their fire.

The orange flames licked up to the heavens. Yellow tongues burst where the dense tangles of decomposed plant matter erupted, the pressurized compost releasing its dormant energy all at once.

The townspeople could feel the heat, but the smoke and stench were carried away by the easterly wind. The blaze that raced away would be stopped at the Red Elm River that spanned its back border. The asphalt double lane highways that flanked the fields would similarly contain it from spreading horizontally. It would be a peaceful razing, nothing of any practical or nostalgic worth in the burn zone.

The town watched the circus of flame with a hushed reverence. Even the boys stopped running around in their endless games of tag, or pulling at the girls' pigtails. They sat on the porch of the corner store, legs dangling off the edge, paying more attention than they did in any subject at school. In their formative years, the apocalypse of fire seared into their soft memories.

"Poor scarecrow. At least now he won't be able to hurt anyone ever again," little red-headed Ricky Moroge announced to no one in particular.

Eyes hidden under the various styles of weathered cowboy hats, the old men shrugged. Sitting shoulder to shoulder, every seat taken, they sipped their beers in silence. Illuminated by the light of the burning field, no one gave a second glance to the ragged old-timer, hat dustier and floppier than any other, with the horribly straight spine and frayed grin.

## About the Author

S.E. Casey grew up in New England near a lighthouse. He always dreamed of smashing the lighthouse and building something truly grotesque with the rubble. This is the writing method for his existential tales focused on a tragic collection of flawed oddities, forgotten places, and fallen characters. His stories have or are scheduled to be published in many magazines, anthologies, and online publications such as Devolution Z, Weirdbook,

Deadman's Tome *Monsters Exist*, Molotov Cocktail Lit Zine, Aphotic Realm, in addition to his own short story collection, *Stygian Doorways.*

Website:
www.secaseyauthor.wordpress.com

# AFTERWORD

Twenty stories down! Did you have a favorite? Each one of these authors puts their all into their craft. Day in and day out--these authors wake up, go to their day job, take care of families, and still cram in time to do what they love.

We included the bio for each author after their stories, I implore you to step out and support those authors that tickled your fancy. Grab one of their collections or another magazine they've been published in--every little gesture is greatly appreciated.

If you haven't had a chance to check out our latest of our quarterly magazines, we just released issue 3 themed CLASSIFIED! Featuring an interview with Mylo Carbia, "The Queen of Horror." Her breakout novel, *The Raping of Ava DeSantis*, quickly topped the charts as the number 1 best selling book and won numerous awards in the matter of days. Another highlight from CLASSIFIED is the interview with Richard Chizmar, founder of the long running horror magazine, Cemetery Dance, best selling co-author of Gwendy's Button Box and Widow's Point. I got to sit down with them and talk all things HORROR.

As always, we'd like to send a big thank you out into the Realm for YOU. Thank you for purchasing this collection and supporting all that we do. Aphotic Realm isn't finished. We're just getting started.

Thank you,

Dustin

**Your Aphotic Realm Team**

**Dustin Schyler Yoak**

**A.A. Medina**

**Chris Martin**

**Gunnar Larsen**

APHOTIC REALM
STRANGE AND SINISTER FICTION MAGAZINE
APPARITIONS

APHOTIC REALM
STRANGE AND SINISTER FICTION MAGAZINE
BANISHED

www.AphoticRealm.com

APHOTIC REALM
STRANGE AND SINISTER FICTION MAGAZINE
FEATURED INTERVIEWS
MYLO CARBIA
&
RICHARD CHIZMAR
CLASSIFIED
ONE YEAR ANNIVERSARY ISSUE

SHADOWS
OF THE MIND

Made in the USA
San Bernardino, CA
04 May 2018